Text Classics

T0363046

HELEN GARNER was born in 1942 in Geelong, and was educated there and at Melbourne University. She taught in Victorian secondary schools until 1972, when she was dismissed for answering her students' questions about sex, and started writing journalism for a living.

Her first novel, *Monkey Grip*, came out in 1977, won the 1978 National Book Council Award and was adapted for film in 1981. Since then she has published novels, short stories, essays and feature journalism. Her screenplays *Two Friends* and *The Last Days of Chez Nous* were filmed in 1986 and 1992, respectively.

In 1995 she published *The First Stone*, a controversial account of a Melbourne University sexual-harassment case. *Joe Cinque's Consolation* (2004) was a study of two murder trials in Canberra. Her account of the trial of Robert Farquharson, *This House of Grief* (2014), was a *Times Literary Supplement* Book of the Year and won the Ned Kelly Award for Best True Crime Book. Her most recent novel, *The Spare Room* (2008), was translated into many languages, and won a Victorian Premier's Literary Award, a Queensland Premier's Award and the Barbara Jefferis Award.

Garner has also won a Walkley Award, in 1993; the inaugural Melbourne Prize for Literature, in 2006; and the Windham–Campbell Prize for Non-Fiction, in 2016. Her latest book, *Everywhere I Look* (2016), is a collection of non-fiction. She lives in Melbourne.

LAURA JONES is a screenwriter whose feature-film credits include *An Angel at My Table*, *Oscar and Lucinda*, *High Tide*, *The Well* and *The Portrait of a Lady*. She received the Australian Writers' Guild Inaugural Lifetime Achievement Award in 2016.

ALSO BY HELEN GARNER

FICTION

Monkey Grip

Honour and Other People's Children

The Children's Bach

Postcards from Surfers

Cosmo Cosmolino

The Spare Room

NON-FICTION

The First Stone

True Stories

The Feel of Steel

Joe Cinque's Consolation

This House of Grief

Everywhere I Look

The Last Days of Chez Nous
& Two Friends
Helen Garner

Text Publishing Melbourne Australia

textclassics.com.au
textpublishing.com.au

The Text Publishing Company
Swann House
22 William Street
Melbourne Victoria 3000
Australia

First published by McPhee Gribble, an imprint of Penguin Books Australia, 1992
This edition published by The Text Publishing Company 2016

Cover design by WH Chong
Typeset by Midland Typesetters

Printed in Australia by Griffin Press, an Accredited ISO AS/NZS 14001:2004
Environmental Management System printer

Primary print ISBN: 9781925355635
Ebook ISBN: 9781925410068
Creator: Garner, Helen, 1942– author.
Title: The last days of chez nous, and, Two friends / by Helen Garner;
afterword by Laura Jones.
Series: Text classics.
Dewey Number: 791.4375

CONTENTS

The Last Days of Chez Nous
& Two Friends

PREFACE

You can write a whole novel with your left arm curved round the page. You can get to the end of the last draft without having shown it to a single person or made one compromise. Even if you have to battle with an editor, the book reaches the reader pretty much as you intended it. All its mistakes and failures are yours, totally and forever, and so are its little glories. When the chips are down, you are the book, and the book is you.

Why would a novelist turn her back on this marvellous freedom, this privacy and independence, and sneak into the bunfight of screenwriting?

I did it for the money. That was my first reason, anyway. At a friend's wedding I met a producer I liked who asked me to contact her if I ever felt like writing a movie. Naïvely, and being broke at the time, I rushed home and rummaged in my folder of unexamined ideas. Out of it stepped Kelly and Louise, the young girls who became *Two Friends*.

But within a week I realised that though the money is a spur, it's also only a mirage, once you've sat down at the desk. I found that film writing is powered by the same drives as fiction. You do it out of curiosity, and technical fascination, and the same old need to shape life's mess into a seizable story.

I've seen a lot of movies, but I hadn't a clue how to write a screenplay. The formal stages of its development—outline, treatment, drafts—were utterly foreign to me. When I write a novel or a story, I never plan. I circle round the dark area of life (mine, or someone else's) to which my curiosity is attracted, and I search for a way in. My method of work is a kind of blind scrub-bashing, a blundering through a trackless forest.

But now I found I was required to sit up brightly in a watchtower and tap out a preliminary map of the territory. I had to turn my old, organic, secretive, privileged, hyper-sensitive work process inside out.

This was the hardest part of the change, for me. I'm used to working alone. It suits my nature. I can't stand it if anyone (no matter how dear) comes into the room behind me while I'm working. I have to cover the pathetic, scrambled mess on the page. I like to get the thing as perfect as I can make it, before I hand it over.

With movies, this won't wash. I had to learn to walk into someone else's room, whack down my idea like a lump of raw meat, and watch it quiver while it was rolled and prodded on the table.

This might easily have been as gruesome as it sounds; but in fact my brief experience of filmwriting has been an intense pleasure, because of the calibre of the people who introduced me to it: Jan Chapman, who produced both these films, and the directors Jane Campion (*Two Friends*) and Gillian Armstrong (*The Last Days of Chez Nous*). Long script sessions with these three classy, generous and challenging professionals taught me to drop my defensiveness and become more flexible at an earlier stage, before my thoughts could set themselves in concrete. They showed me the priceless art of the apparently dumb question, and the calm brazenness that is required in order to ask it. From Gillian Armstrong I learnt that before you can cut something out of the story you have to understand fully what it is, instead of dropping it because you're too lazy to think it right through. I learnt (from Jane Campion in particular) to follow and trust intuition, no matter how alarmingly it swerves. And most valuably of all, because it applies to everything written in any genre, all three of them forced me to learn and relearn the stern law of structure.

What I had seen, in a late draft of *Chez Nous* for example, as a perfectly smooth narrative curve would turn out, under their skilful probing, to be more like a little Himalaya of mini-climaxes. Special effects a novelist might pull off on the page by bluff or flashy language simply will not transpose to film. Everything has to be reinvented through the eyes. It was very squashing to have to leave my precious prose at the door and be pushed back again and again to the bare bones of structure and dialogue. There *is* nothing else, it seemed at times. So hard, to be so stripped!

But there's a payoff: how shockingly easy it is just to write 'Night, a desert motel', or 'She takes her father's arm', and to leave the rest, the complex labour of providing the detail that will fill the bare places and acts with meaning, to the director's incredibly numerous and expensive army of actors and technicians. The ease of it—it seemed criminal; I felt almost guilty.

Does anyone understand the alchemy of many imaginations that distils a film? An actor's mistaken emphasis can throw a carefully crafted piece of psychology out of whack. The wrong brand of teacup on a table can skew a family's fantasy of itself. But by the same token, the tiny upward movement of one facial muscle, spontaneous, unconscious, impossible to write, can transform the emotional mood of an entire sequence. A director can take hold of your stick of an idea and make it blossom into a poetry your plodding typewriter could never have dreamt of.

I've read the horror stories and I know how lucky I've been. At the start I was hampered by a pathetic gratitude that my work was even considered filmable. I didn't (and still don't) understand the writer's position and power in the hierarchy of the production army. I was often too proud to ask the dumb question that would have taught me what I needed to know. I discovered in myself a passivity I never knew was there. I stayed away while the films were being shot, and when you're not present, when you're in another town, everything you think is always too late. I accepted without a struggle, over the phone, last-minute changes the necessity of which I was too inexperienced to judge. I still haven't learnt how—and when—to fight for what I see as crucial. I haven't yet learnt to foresee the flashpoints where imagination and budget might collide, and to take a stand long before the moment, on location, when the crucial is found to be impossible and the lesser road must be taken.

In *Chez Nous*, for example, there are the cypress trees.

From the main characters' bedroom window I wanted a row of pencil cypress trees to be visible, growing in a distant and unidentifiable neighbourhood garden. These trees, to me, carry a heavy freight of meaning. They are Mediterranean, and connected with the origins of our culture. They are calm, sturdy, graceful. They are a reminder of darkness, of stillness, of death—and thus of the question of God, and the soul. At certain charged moments in the plot of *Chez Nous*, people glance out the window and see the cypresses. Once, Beth speaks of them to her pregnant friend in a way that tells us a good deal about her.

In this book you will read about the cypresses. But in the film of *Chez Nous* you will not see them.

When a terrace house in Glebe was chosen for the film, it was perfect in every way except one: there were no cypress trees. The cypress trees, it seemed, would not be possible. I went to the house with Jan Chapman and Gillian Armstrong, and we walked from window to window, looking for something to replace them. Then, from an upstairs room we saw, beyond the thick summer foliage into which the house backed, the tip of a church spire, just floating there. The building to which it was attached was completely hidden by leafy branches. At that anxious moment it seemed a gift, and we persuaded ourselves that the spire would do.

And in a sense it did do—but a resonance departed. A spire, no matter how indistinct and beautiful, is literal. It represents a known religion, a particular theology, with all the sectarian and social meanings that this entails. The mystery of the image is lost. So in this book I have taken the liberty of removing the spire, and putting the cypress trees back in.

The qualities of air and light in a certain place, I now realise, are more than simply aesthetic. They form the tone of people's lives, the way people move about and behave towards each other and feel about themselves. Both these films were imagined in Melbourne and shot in Sydney. I didn't think this would matter, but the experience has taught me that the two big cities of Australia are tonally as distinct from each other as Boston is from LA, or Lyon from Marseilles. The very image of *a house,* on which both films heavily depend, bears one sort of psychological emphasis in warm, open Sydney, and a completely different one in Melbourne, where dwellings are enclosing, curtained, cold-weather-resisting: more like burrows.

These are only a few of the lessons I have learnt. I don't know yet whether I will have another chance at applying them to a film. I think I will always prefer to write fiction. Collaboration, if you're used to the long spells of obsessive loneliness that fiction demands, is weirdly over-exciting. You go home each day suspecting that you have made a complete fool of yourself. It feels illicit. All that laughter!

Can this really be work? People hang around whose job is to *bring you a cup of tea*! A sandwich on a plate! And to clear away the crockery afterwards while you go on talking! You are afraid of being swallowed up by the seductive machinery of it, the intricate balancing of forces that you barely understand.

And as for the money—the appalling sums it *costs*, to make your ideas visible—I will never get used to this. Thinking about it nearly makes me keel over. Yes, at the beginning I really thought I was doing it for the money. But now I know that if I do it again, it will be for the slightly crazed pleasure of collaboration, and for the subtle little quiver of possibility that the enterprise gives off at the start—the distant flicker of a not yet perfected story that might end up satisfying and deep, if the chemistry is right. And, of course, for the moment when you sit down in the dark and see your characters walk and talk, with tones in their voices and expressions on their faces; when you see them spin away from you and out into the world of strangers.

Helen Garner
Melbourne, 1992

THE LAST DAYS
OF CHEZ NOUS

screenplay by
HELEN GARNER

directed by
GILLIAN ARMSTRONG

produced by
JAN CHAPMAN

CAST LIST

BETH	Lisa Harrow
JP	Bruno Ganz
VICKI	Kerry Fox
ANNIE	Miranda Otto
TIM	Kiri Paramore
BETH'S FATHER	Bill Hunter
ANGELO	Lex Marinos
SALLY	Mickey Camilleri
BETH'S MOTHER	Lynne Murphy
PENNY	Claire Haywood
SUSIE	Leanne Bundy
CAFÉ DERO	Wilson Alcorn
THIEF	Tom Weaver
MAYOR	Bill Brady
WAITRESS	Eva di Cesare
WAITER	Tony Poli
SINGING WOMAN	Olga Sanderson
CLINIC NURSE	Joyce Hopwood
STRANGER	Steve Cox
OLD MAN DESERT TOURIST	Harry Griffiths
DESERT WAITRESS	Amanda Martin

MAIN CHARACTERS

JP 40s, a Frenchman living in Australia
BETH 40s, his Australian wife
ANNIE 16, Beth's daughter from
a previous marriage
VICKI 25, Beth's youngest sister
TIM 19, a student boarder with the family
BETH'S FATHER 70
ANGELO 40, a friend of Beth and JP
SALLY 38, married to Angelo,
also a friend of the family

NOTE

The house in which the film was shot has an outside stair-case: to get from the ground floor to the upper storey, where the bathroom and all the bedrooms (except Vicki's) are, people have to go out the back door and through the yard. A verandah runs along the back and side of the top storey, overlooking the yard.

It is late on a summer afternoon. Vicki, the worse for travel, is trudging up the lane behind the house, dragging behind her a suitcase on wheels, and carrying several smaller bags. She opens the gate with a key, and crosses the yard, lumping the luggage behind her; she goes through the open back door and into the dining room.

VICKI: Yoo hoo!

Silence. Nobody home.

On the table stands a heart-shaped cake, home-made and luridly iced by someone eager and not very skilful.

Vicki dumps her bags, grabs a big knife off the sideboard (she is clearly at home here), cuts herself a huge slab of the cake, and walks away into the house eating it.

She enters her own bedroom, which is off the living room. It is empty of everything except a bed, table and chair, but it's clean, and the bed is made up with fresh sheets, one corner turned back welcomingly, a bunch of flowers in a jar on the table, a towel folded on the end of the bed. A piece of Caneite is fixed to the wall with photos and cuttings pinned to it: this has been here a long time, left over from her previous occupancy of the room.

She stands there looking round, still chewing the lump of cake. Approaches the Caneite board and examines the photos. These include a newspaper cutting (yellowing) with a headline about a prize and a photo of Beth behind a typewriter; but more importantly at this moment, a colour photo of a young man. Still eating, Vicki reaches out one hand and carefully unpins the young man's photo from the board. Holding the piece of cake in her mouth, she uses two hands to tear the photo methodically into many pieces.

She comes out of her room, and retraces her steps across the dining room and out into the yard.

She starts up the back stairs. Halfway up, a moment of wooziness makes her clutch at the handrail and pause, but she gets control of herself and continues to climb the stairs, chewing and swallowing the last mouthful.

She walks along the upper hall and pokes her head into Annie's bedroom: a glimpse of teenage chaos, though rather bookish.

Next she opens the door of the main bedroom, JP and Beth's room. She goes in.

The man's side of the room is messy, as if a boy lived in it: dirty runners, a tennis racquet, newspapers strewn around. The woman's side by comparison is prim, almost bare: it looks recently organised and tidied. In an alcove off the room stands a table with a typewriter on it, and piles of paper. None of her clothes are lying about.

15

Vicki approaches the bed, and with a strange sigh casts herself on to it. She presses her face into Beth's pillow. She relaxes. Then suddenly she leaps up and bolts out of the room with her hand over her mouth.

In the bathroom Vicki wipes her mouth as she straightens up from the toilet into which she has just been sick. She flushes it.

Screeches are heard from the kitchen below.

ANNIE: Vicki! Vicki!

Vicki rinses her mouth at the basin and, wiping her face, darts out into the hallway.

VICKI: I'm up here.

Downstairs in the dining room, Beth approaches the table and sees the cake has been broached. Annie is running out the back door towards the stairs, yelling, in great excitement.

ANNIE: Where are you?

Downstairs, Beth picks up two oranges from the fruit bowl.

Annie and Vicki come tumbling down the stairs towards the back door.

VICKI: I had to get the *bus*!

ANNIE: You said Friday—I'm *sure* you said Friday.

Beth is standing in the back doorway, striking a crass pose with the oranges stuffed down her jumper and holding the cake on its plate.

BETH (*in coarse Australian accent*): Okay—which of youse two molls got stuck into this cake?

VICKI (*bursts out laughing*): The Butterworths!

BETH: Cheryl Butterworth is still top dog round here.

Beth lets the oranges drop out of the front of her jumper. She and Vicki fall into each other's arms. Vicki is almost crying. She wipes her eyes furtively behind her sister's shoulder as they embrace.

VICKI: Ah, Beth—I haven't had a good laugh since I left.

BETH: Don't they talk dirty in Wogland?

VICKI: I brought you some stuff.

A great fuss of cake-eating and parcel-opening: New York-style presents, cheap vulgar funny things—toys, in fact—including a grotesque pair of rubber gloves with red fingernails and a crude metal ring on the wedding finger.

17

ANNIE (*seizing gloves—teasingly*): Hey! Vicki got married!

This is a clanger but Vicki responds by grabbing the gloves back.

VICKI: No! They're for *Beth*!

ANNIE (*unaware of her tactlessness*): We need another man round here. The Butterworths need boyfriends.

VICKI: Blokes can't play Butterworths. It's a girls' game.

ANNIE: What about that cupboard upstairs. Someone could pay rent. A student.

BETH: It'd have to be an Australian. One wog's plenty.

VICKI: Where is he?

ANNIE: We should have waited with the cake.

They start to giggle. Annie tries to make the cake remains look more presentable.
There is a rattle of hubcaps in the street.
Vicki runs to the front door, and out on to the verandah.
On the street in front of the house, JP gets out of a dinted Kingswood and locks it.

VICKI: (*leaning over the railing in Butterworth style*): G'day dago. You still here?

18

JP (*tries to answer in Butterworth voice*): Moll. You are already back. Where 'ave you bin?

VICKI (*Butterworth style*): None of your business.

They are both straight-faced but it is a joking exchange.

———————————

The same evening JP and Beth are preparing dinner, cheerfully, moving closely and with familiarity in the small kitchen. JP wields a meat cleaver, singing.

JP (*with gusto*): 'Nessun dorma...nessun dormammmm...'

BETH (*absentmindedly critical*): You always go *mmmm* when you sing.

JP: Tu sais rien du tout. C'est comme ça qu'il faut chanter. (*What would you know? That's the right way to sing.*)

Vicki is leaning in the back doorway, holding a newspaper in one hand but looking out into the yard and beyond.

JP (*pleasantly to Vicki*): Do you want a little job to do?

VICKI (*taking no notice; in a jetlag reverie*): I was watching the light change on the Simeonis' place.

BETH (*working; without looking up*): There was practically murder over there while you were away.

JP (*acting; raising the cleaver*): 'You will go to this wedding over my dead body.'

BETH (*in her brisk, rather tough manner*): Someone pregnant who shouldn't have been, I suppose. Look out— your oil's burning. You'd think girls these days would have more sense.

Vicki reads aloud from the paper in the doorway while the others work.

VICKI: It says here that there are more than a million and a half stray cats in this city.

Vicki wanders away into the living room.

JP (*unaggressively; just remarking*): Elle fout rien, ta soeur. (*She never lifts a finger, your sister.*)

BETH (*lightly defensive of Vicki*): Tu es pire que mon père. (*You're worse than my father.*) She's only just got off the plane.

That evening. The table is set and at it sit Beth, Annie and Vicki, waiting to be served. Through the living room we can see that the front door is still wide open on to the street. JP enters the dining room, ceremoniously bearing a large dish.

JP: Mesdames; le plat de résistance.

ANNIE (*to tease: they are fond of each other*): Don't talk wog.

BETH (*in loud, commanding tone*): The mat, the mat—put it on the mat.

She forces a mat under the hot dish. No one takes any notice of Beth when she talks like this: it's her way, they are used to it.

Phone rings in the living room.

BETH (*in loud, fast voice, as if it's always for her*): I'll get it.

Beth darts out of the room.

The others serve themselves and eat. Annie has a folder beside her and keeps riffling through her notes while she eats, mouthing things she is learning by heart, putting on an act of 'the intolerable burden' of the final year of high school.

JP (*mildly to Vicki*): And what are you going to do, now you are back 'ome?

21

VICKI (*with a vague defensiveness*): Oh…fix up my room…

JP: Non! With your life!

VICKI (*writhing, as if pressured by a parent*): I don't know!
    Go on the dole, I suppose, till I…

Beth rushes back in and picks up her fork again with vigour, cutting straight across their conversation.

BETH: You'd think they could let me have a meal in peace.

JP: Why don't we pull the phone out of the wall?

BETH (*briskly brushing this aside*): It might be important.

JP sits back. When squashed like this, his face closes.

ANNIE: There's that lady again.

They listen, forks raised.

On the other side of the street in the dark, a woman in a pleated skirt, with a fat bum, glasses, a modest middle-aged haircut, carrying a briefcase, is walking past along the pavement on her way home. She is singing in a strong, confident but not trained voice—an alto, a womanly, *adult* voice—'Why do the nations so furiously rage together?' She does not care that it is a man's song. She is singing for her own pleasure, unaware that she is being listened to.

JP (*to Vicki, trying to revive the previous topic*): You are a clever girl. You can get a job without problems.

VICKI: I'm not a *girl*.

BETH: She's not a *girl*. } simultaneously

Beth and Vicki laugh, looking at each other. A minor ganging-up against JP, who looks away, feeling the exclusion.

The phone rings. Beth rushes to answer it.

The woman's singing is meanwhile fading in the distance.

The others eat, looking down.

Later the same night, Beth and Vicki are washing up together. They are making each other laugh, falling about foolishly as they work. They are addicted to each other's sense of the ridiculous.

VICKI: She wore these terrible shoes. They looked like two crows' beaks.

They laugh wildly, disproportionately.

VICKI: And she told me they got married so they could stay in a motel without having to tell a lie.

They are light-headed, giggling like girls.

BETH: Start writing it, Vicki. Start tomorrow.

VICKI (*sobering up*): But how do I know whether I'll ever be any good?

BETH: You don't. Just start.

VICKI (*with light resentment, turning away*): It's all right for *you*.

Early next morning.

JP and Beth are in bed asleep. An alarm goes off: ABC voice in mid-sentence reading the bad news. Beth wakes first. She looks at JP while he sleeps: a quiet scrutiny. In sleep, his hands are clasped under his chin. He wakes.

JP (*thickly*): Quelle heure il est?

BETH: You had your hands clasped, like this—as if you were praying.

JP: I have not won the Lotto? You have not had a proper haircut? There is no God.

Beth hangs on to his back as they lie there.

BETH: Shouldn't we get up?

JP: In one minute.

Steps run along the hall; a door slams.

JP: Oh merde. Your bloody sister.

BETH: Vicki's tougher, don't you think?

JP (*eyes still closed*): She is still 'opeless. Spoilt like a baby.

BETH (*fondly*): I'm so glad she's back. I missed her.

JP (*unaggressively*): You missed your mirror. You missed your little echo. One day this girl will have to break from you.

Beth laughs. She rubs her front against his back, but he makes no response. She accepts this philosophically, with a sigh.

BETH (*in mock gloom*): Do you think we'll ever make love again?

JP (*nonplussed*): Why do you say this? C'est pas la question qu'il faut poser. (*It's not the right question to ask.*)

He heaves himself out of bed, grabs a towel and puts it round him; walks to the door, still stunned with sleep. Behind his back Beth sticks her tongue out at him with childish violence. He goes out.

BETH (*to no one*): What *is* the right question?

Sound of JP banging on the bathroom door and yelling impatiently.

JP: Vicki!

Morning. Beth comes whirling out the door on to the upstairs verandah, carrying a plastic bag stuffed with folders and an exercise book. Her friend Sal, hugely pregnant, is seated in the sun at the top of the stairs, beside a pot of rosemary.

BETH: Don't settle in, Sal. I've got to photocopy.

Sal makes as if to stand up, then hesitates.

SALLY: Ooh. He kicked.

BETH: Or she.

SALLY: I'm not supposed to tell, but it's a boy. At my age they test you for everything.

Beth is all revved up to start the day, but she is fond of Sal and pauses, though still on her feet, to weed the rosemary in the pot. Her movements are brisk and short, while Sal is slower and more tranquil.

BETH: I'm glad I did it while I was still too silly to know better.

SALLY: Get your tubes fixed and have another one.

BETH: Me?

SALLY: That's what JP needs.

Beth gives a light laugh, as at a casual remark. Pause.

BETH (*weeding vigorously*): …Vicki's back.

SALLY: I thought there was some bloke. In Italy.

BETH: It fell through.

SALLY: Is she miserable?

BETH: Hard to tell.

Beth tears off a bunch of rosemary and hands it to Sal who sniffs at it.

27

SALLY: Angelo says rosemary only grows where a woman's in control.

Beth laughs through her nose, concentrating on what she's doing.

SALLY (*placidly, looking over Beth's head at a distant garden*): Those cypress trees are beautiful, aren't they. Like a hand held up.

Beth wipes her hands on her skirt and sets off down the stairs in a work-going manner. Sally heaves herself to her feet and slowly follows.

BETH (*over her shoulder as she descends*): I always think I should find out whose garden they're in. I've been up and down those lanes, and I can never find them. I set off in a really businesslike way, but pretty soon I start worrying about something else, and by the time I get to the corner I've forgotten what I was looking for.

They both laugh. Beth surges out of the gate and disappears. Left behind, Sal follows slowly, and carefully pulls the gate shut after her.

———————

Late one afternoon, some days later, the three women are in the living room. Beth is ironing. Annie is doing maths with a calculator. Vicki is wandering aimlessly, looking at herself in the glass of a picture on the wall.

VICKI: This haircut's *over*.

BETH: You worry too much. Annie, run the hoover over this carpet will you, sweetheart?

ANNIE: Tell Vicki to. I'm working.

Vicki takes no notice, examining herself discontentedly. She drifts away across the dining room and into the backyard.

BETH: I'm asking *you* to.

ANNIE: But why. I'm the one with exams. You never ask her to do anything.

BETH: Yes I do.

ANNIE: But you never make her.

BETH: Make her? I'm not her mother.

ANNIE: Why doesn't she go home to grandma and grandpa then?

VICKI (*loudly, coming back in*): Because they're too old. They were too old when they had me and they're too old to tell things to.

Pause. This is convincing.

Idle and bored, Vicki opens the drawer of the sideboard and rummages among the mess of revolting old worn-out lipsticks, rubber bands, packs of cards, false nose-and-spectacles, etc.; also a piece of plastic dog shit left over from some joke.

Vicki chooses a lipstick stub and smears it on her mouth; looks at herself in the glass.

VICKI: JP's got balder, hasn't he.

BETH (*ironing*): Balding men are sexy.

VICKI (*launching the Butterworth game*): You'd know, Cheryl.

BETH: I would, too. I been around.

ANNIE (*joining in*): Ewww. You're slack.

BETH (*as Cheryl*): Don't take that tone to *me*, Tiffany Butterworth. Show some respect.

ANNIE: You *are*—isn't she, Chantelle. You're *rough*.

BETH (*ironing with increasing vigour*): You can talk that way now, my girl, but once you get out into the world of men and have to hawk y' fork I bet you'll change your tune.

ANNIE (*with gusto*): I will not. I'm never gunna be like you. You're a moll.

Vicki, with one hand full of old make-up, seizes Annie by the shoulder with the other and spins her round in the chair.

VICKI: Come on, Mum. We'll show her what it means to be a real woman.

Beth leaves the iron standing on the board and joins in. She and Vicki fall on Annie and transform her into a moll; all the while they are talking and murmuring, as below. Annie, still playing Tiffany, submits to this. They are all hamming it up as Butterworths, holding back laughter, but in fact it is a distorted initiation ceremony in which Vicki is expressing obliquely what happened to her overseas; there is also a hidden sadism in the process (as in all initiation ceremonies)—revenge on Annie for her youth and innocence; and for the jealousy Annie has expressed of Vicki's use of Beth as an indulgent mother.

BETH: I could tell you girls a thing or two about men.

ANNIE (*cheekily*): I bet you could.

BETH: Don't move your mouth.

VICKI: They're only after one thing, aren't they, Cheryl.

BETH: That's right, darl. And when they've had it they throw you away.

ANNIE: Ow. *Ow*.

BETH: Shutup Tiff. A girl has to *suffer,* to be beautiful.

VICKI: Show up them cheekbones, love.

BETH: If you got it, flaunt it.

VICKI: Come on—pout. *Pout*.

BETH: Make 'em *quiver*. That's right.

VICKI: Isn't her skin gorgeous.

BETH (*grimly*): Not for long.

The iron stands upright on the board, emitting faint hisses and puffs of steam.

A head shot of the transformed girl. A horrible sight. Silence.

Annie hops up and darts out of the room to look at herself upstairs.

VICKI (*turns to Beth in a rush*): I think I'm pregnant.

Beth's expression: surprise, pleasure, envy.

VICKI: I *am*. Don't you tell anyone.

BETH: What are you going to do?

VICKI (*ignoring the question*): I know what you think. And don't you dare tell Dad.

BETH: What do you *take* me for?

VICKI: And don't tell JP, either.

BETH: Why would I tell JP?

VICKI: Don't married people tell each other everything?

Beth gives her a cynical look and says nothing.

———————————

Some days later, Beth is standing on the upstairs verandah with Tim, a young student, a likely candidate for the room the family wants to let. They are looking through the door into the room, which is rather bare; but Tim seems interested.

BETH: Will you need a table?

TIM: I study in bed.

BETH: One last question. Have you got a sense of humour?

TIM (*with a slightly mystified shrug*): I think so.

Sunday morning in the living room. Opera is blasting away on the stereo. JP and Annie are playing a game, trying to throw a beret like a frisbee so that it lands on the other person's head. JP is throwing. Annie keeps jumping up on an angle with her arms straight along her sides, trying to get her head under the flying beret. They are weak with laughter.

JP: Tu fais des petits bonds ridicules. (*You do these silly little jumps.*) Stay still! Let *me* do the work!

Tim enters shyly; he sees them and looks amazed. They take no notice. Beth rushes in, wearing a striped French cotton jumper the same as the one JP is wearing. He notices this, points it out and laughs.

BETH (*firmly, to JP*): You'll have to get changed.

JP (*indignant*): Mais c'est *moi* le Français! (*But* I'm *the Frenchman!*)

The phone rings.

BETH (*rushing to answer it*): Come on—we're late. Mum'll have a fit.

34

JP throws the beret straight up in the air and tries to crown himself with it. Tim shoulders him out of the way and gets *his* head under the flying beret.

Later that morning, in the kitchen at the house of Beth's and Vicki's parents. Their mother and JP are standing at the bench. JP (not wearing stripes) is mixing up a vinaigrette with flair. Mother watches admiringly, though she knows perfectly well how to do it herself.

JP: At Christmas, Susie had buffet. I don't like so much buffet. People should sit all at one table. Someone tells a story—everybody laughs.

MOTHER: Doug's not mad keen on formality. He says it slows everything down. When we went on our cruise—

JP (*cutting across her gently, as across someone who habitually raves on pointlessly*): An' I like spitches. When someone stands up and makes a spitch.

MOTHER: Oh, I don't think Doug would agree with you there. He's been known to fall asleep at the bowling club dinner.

JP: But why? Why are Australians so casual?

MOTHER: It's just our way, dear. We like to feel at ease.

JP: But even when you raise the glass to say 'Cheers', you don't look the other people in the eyes.

MOTHER: Ooh! I've never noticed that.

JP: Where I work, everyone is a wog. Most days we eat our lunch together. At a table. But out the window I see people from the other buildings—it's sad—they go outside and sit each one alone with his sandwich.

Meanwhile, in the lounge room, Annie is sitting in a corner bent over a folder of notes. Beth (wearing stripes) is setting the table, and to amuse Vicki, who has paused beside her on her way across the room carrying a comb standing up in a glass of water, she lays in their father's place at the table a huge salad bowl and huge salad servers, instead of the usual implements that she has laid in all the other places. They giggle silently.

BETH (*whispering*): Have you rung the clinic yet?

Without answering, Vicki walks across towards their father who is sitting on the couch reading the paper with his back to the room. She begins to comb his hair with the wet comb.

FATHER (*eyes closed*): Very nice, missy. Why haven't the others come down?

BETH (*calling out officiously*): Susie and Penny'll be here in a minute. Clare's mad at you for the way you yelled at her on the phone. Bill's working, and Sandy can't go anywhere for a week because she put henna in her hair and it went orange.

Father and Vicki exchange an expressionless glance. Father's eyes close again, and Vicki goes on rhythmically combing.

———————————

Now the meal is almost over. At the table are Beth, JP, Annie, Vicki, Mother, Father, Susie and Penny. Mother starts to serve out the dessert, a large bowl of raspberries.

FATHER: Vicki used to call 'em rise-berries, remember?

BETH: You always remember *her* cute sayings.

VICKI (*cheekily*): Yours were so long ago, everybody's forgotten them.

FATHER: No we haven't. Remember when I pointed out two Chinamen to you, Beth? And you said—

BETH and FATHER (*in chorus*): 'When do they chine?'

Beth and Father laugh, looking at each other, but suddenly his attention switches to Mother's distribution of fruit, though only with the size of his own serve in mind.

FATHER: Ay, ay. Come on, Mum. Be fair.

BETH (*cross again already, standing up*): There's plenty, Dad.

Mother does not even bother to reply; she has the flattened and stoical manner of Australian mothers of her generation.

VICKI (*sitting beside her father in favourite-girl mode*): Hey, Annie! Look! A great big spider.

Annie falls for it and looks up at the ceiling. Vicki grabs and eats a raspberry from her bowl. Annie gives a cry of protest.

VICKI (*chewing luxuriously; looks up at Father*): I learnt that trick from you.

Father stands up in his place and reaches across people to get the jug of cream. A great feminine chorus of objection.

MOTHER: No, Doug!

BETH: Put that down!

SUSIE: You're not allowed!

VICKI: You're supposed to lose weight!

BETH: Don't be such a pig!

MOTHER: Look at that stomach!

But JP jumps up, dashes to Father's side and holds up his serviette like a little curtain behind which Father, with a smug smile, lavishes cream upon his bowl of fruit.

It is hours later, in the middle of a summer afternoon. In the foreground, the father has fallen asleep on the sofa: he lies curled up on his side; the newspaper drops from his hand. In the background, all the others are still at the table. The meal is over but they have been talking.

Beth and Vicki, spontaneously and unconsciously in unison, stand up from the table and turn away from it in opposite directions, while raising both hands to lift their hair off their necks: in this gesture we see that despite the difference in their ages they strongly resemble each other.

It is the evening of the same day. JP and Beth are walking home from the shop, carrying plastic bags full of shopping. They are companionable, if not intimate.

JP: This girl has been to Chicago, New York, Rome by herself and still you say 'She needs me'!

BETH (*slightly abashed*): She thinks my jokes are funny.

JP: She copies you. Can't you see this? She follows your opinions.

BETH: Oh! *I* thought we just agreed on everything naturally.

JP: At least she will not copy this trip with your father.

BETH: You think it's silly, don't you.

JP: Not silly, but—(*blows out air*)—three weeks! Driving driving—only you and him—you will murder each other. Take someone else. Take your mother.

BETH: But the whole point of it is *not* to take my mother. It's got to be just him and me. One to one.

JP laughs at her heroic tone.

JP: Will you take a tent? Or sleep under the sky?

BETH (*embarrassed to confess*): He likes motels.

JP (*with distaste*): Motels. Oh là là.

BETH (*urgently, wanting him not to criticise*): He's old, see. I'm scared he'll die before I can—

JP: Before what?

BETH: Before I can get things sorted out.

JP: You have this mania for resolution. With you everything must be—

He makes a squaring-off gesture, a *chopping* gesture, with two hands.

BETH: Well. I dared him to go. I can't back out now.

JP (*putting his arm around her shoulders*): You are a crazy woman.

BETH (*so absorbed in her own plans, she hardly notices his affection*): I can wear my new boots!

JP removes his arm and mimics her gait, mincing in heavy walking boots, primly pursing his lips.

JP: 'My new boots.'

They laugh. Beth picks up a lump of wood off the pavement and brandishes it.

BETH: At least I don't wear ugg boots, like whatsername. Your teenage friend. I bet she sucked your cock, didn't she.

JP (*examining his fingernails with provocative smugness*): Et alors? (*So?*)

BETH: You bastard.

She runs at him with the lump of wood. They are silly with laughter; he dodges her, feinting with the shopping bag.

JP: And *your* boyfriend? With 'is Drizabone and 'is stupid 'at?

She gets serious with the log now, she really wants to hurt him and he bolts away from her, but she catches up with him, waving the wood, and in a spasm of real fear he turns and kicks her in the shin with his big shoe. Game over.

———————————

A week or so later, Vicki is standing sideways in front of the bathroom mirror, parting her shirt and trousers to see whether her stomach has started to bulge yet. It hasn't, but she is looking anxiously.

———————————

On the same morning, in the alcove off the bedroom, Beth is working at her typewriter. JP enters with a manuscript he has just finished reading.

BETH (*anxiously*): Did you like it?

JP puts the manuscript on the very edge of the table, lining it up square with the corner, stalling for time.

JP: I know you always want to hear the good things before the criticism, so, yes, it is very well written. It makes you want to read on. You keep turning the pages with interest...but finalement...I prefer more destructive books.

BETH: Destructive.

JP: You have written life the way you wish it would be. People's motivations are honourable. Love exists. There is hope.

BETH: Well, isn't there?

JP (*touching the manuscript*): You don't write about reality. People are more cruel and égoïstes. Life is much blacker than this.

Beth sits in silence, digesting this and trying to 'accept criticism in a spirit of intellectual objectivity' as she knows one should.

BETH: *Vicki* said it 'smashed her illusions'. *She* said it made her angry.

They look at each other for a moment. Then they both laugh, in a brief, helpless way. JP comes forward and kisses her formally on the cheek.

JP (*lightly*): Quand même, c'est très bien. Tu as fait du bon travail. (*Still, it's very good. You've worked well.*)

BETH (*with difficulty; looking up at him*): Will you be proud of me when I've finished it?

JP (*very lightly, on his way out of the room*): Non. Je serai envieux. (*No. I'll be envious.*)

Same morning. As JP enters the living room where Vicki is sitting among the breakfast dishes, smoking and reading the paper, we hear Beth's typewriter start up again at the top of the house.

VICKI: Here's a lady who had a hysterectomy. She took her uterus home with her in a jar so her son and his friends could see it. Then she was going to bury it and plant a tree over it.

JP is standing at the table putting a box of floppy disks into his attaché case, preparing to leave for work.

JP: Is this all you see in the papers? Don't you read the real news?

VICKI: That's pretty real, isn't it?

JP: You know what I mean. I mean politics. Economics. You would think the real world did not exist.

Vicki is sitting on the arm of the chair right beside the open door. At that moment, a stranger, rather decrepit and eccentric, stops outside, puts his forearms on the railing, and addresses Vicki.

STRANGER: 'Scuse me, love. Got a light?

Vicki obliges, looking slightly startled.

STRANGER: Many thanks. God bless.

The stranger wanders away.

JP standing still with his hands in his attaché case, watches this encounter with open mouth.

JP: Who was *that*?

VICKI: *I* dunno! You're supposed to *protect* me from things like that! (*She is challenging him half as a joke.*)

JP (*flabbergasted*): Who—*me*?

VICKI: Yes! You're the man of the house, aren't you?

JP (*with light irony; even a slight bitterness and continuing his preparations for work*): I thought modern

woman are become *independent*. I thought they don't
need protection any more. They are *free*. This is what
I have bin told.

VICKI: That's Beth's opinion. I'm not Beth, you know.

JP does not answer, but clicks his case shut and leaves the
house, picking up something off the sideboard as he passes.

Vicki turns to the Situations Vacant column and takes
a pencil which she runs up and down the ads.

Something brown and flat comes whizzing in through
the door and lands on the paper Vicki is holding. She leaps
up with a screech. It is the piece of plastic dog shit. She
looks up and sees JP grinning at her from beside the car.
Sound of Beth's typewriter banging away upstairs.

Vicki rolls her eyes at JP and makes a gesture in front
of her face, as of tiny fingers madly typing.

JP still grinning, gets into his car, and drives away. The
Italian lady next door, standing on the footpath with her
broom, waves to him as he passes.

Several days later, Beth and Vicki are having a cup of coffee
in the morning, standing up at the kitchen bench.

BETH: Do you want me to ring up *for* you?

VICKI: No. It's all right. I'll do it myself. Thanks.

BETH (*turning to rinse her cup*): You're a great one for dragging the chain—that's why I asked.

VICKI: I'll get round to it.

BETH: It's best not to delay these things, though.

VICKI (*irritated*): I'll *do* it. Don't *worry*.

That evening, just as it's getting dark, JP, Annie and Vicki, all with wet hair from the pool, are bouncing down the street towards the house.

JP is fooling to make them laugh. We see how at ease he is with people younger than himself. He throws his body into exaggerated rock 'n' roll poses like the ones on 1950s record covers. They are all hilarious, rolling home. Vicki runs at JP from behind and springs on to his back; he piggybacks her. Annie pulls at Vicki, half dragging her off, and tries to clamber aboard herself.

Meanwhile, in the kitchen, Beth is cooking an archetypal Australian meal; sausages under the griller, boiling spuds, brussel sprouts. Music comes from the living room: someone is playing the piano.

BETH (*calling out in a bossy, motherly, self-consciously encouraging voice*): That's very nice, sweetheart.

Tim appears at the dining-room door, looking sheepish.

TIM: It's not sweetheart. It's me.

BETH: Oh! Where is everyone?

TIM: They went down to the pool.

The back door bursts open. JP, Vicki and Annie rock in.

ANNIE (*instant demand*): Mum—did you pick up my blazer from the cleaner?

BETH (*without even looking up, answers with smooth efficiency*): It's in your room.

Meanwhile, JP has gone straight to the high shelf and reached up on tiptoe to get a dish off the top of it. He handles the dish as if it bore something precious and rare. He gets it to eye level. On it is a French cheese. Its wrapping has been torn open and some of it has been eaten. He makes a rattling sound of shock and outrage.

JP (*holding dish out to Beth with a movement both challenging and asking for authoritative intervention*): My brie. Someone has opened it.

48

BETH (*casually*): I did. I had a little bit when I got home.

JP (*seriously upset*): You are so greedy! Your family is all the same! Greedy and selfish!

BETH (*surprised by his vehement reaction*): I was hungry.

JP (*wanting her to understand his distress*): Why do you think I have put it up on top of the cupboard?

BETH (*ready to defend herself*): I don't know. Why did you?

JP (*passionately*): Because it has not yet reached its point of maturation!

BETH (*huffy, defensive, unsympathetic*): *Sorry!*

JP dumps the dish on the bench and goes out the back door towards the stairs. Beth shifts things about on the stove. Annie examines the ravaged cheese in a gingerly manner, as if it might bite her. Tim and Vicki stand around looking embarrassed.

———————

Shortly afterwards, Beth approaches the bedroom. JP is standing with his forehead against the window.

BETH (*from the door*): Dinner's ready.

JP (*without turning around*): I am not hungry.

BETH (*in a conciliatory tone*): Won't you eat with us?

JP: I have already said. I am not hungry.

BETH: You're always hungry.

No response. She goes up behind him and touches his arm.

BETH (*more gently, but still with an undertone of suggestion that he is being unreasonable and should get off his high horse*): Come on, JP. It was only cheese.

JP whirls around. He is almost in tears.

JP: 'Only cheese'! Do you know how long it is since I ate this kind of cheese? Since two years I am looking for it in *every shop*.

BETH: Oh. I didn't realise.

JP (*full of sadness and hurt*): No. You *don't* realise.

Beth is silent. They stand looking at each other. She has not quite succumbed, but for once he has her full attention—and this is so rare that he does not know what to do with it. He hesitates. The phone rings.

Beth looks around sharply. JP turns his head away.

Down in the yard, Annie is yelling towards the stairs, straight past Beth who is hurrying down to answer the phone call.

ANNIE: 'Joan-Pier'! (*She mocks the caller's mispronunciation of his name.*) Phone for you. Some girl.

Half an hour later, Beth, Annie, Vicki and Tim are finishing their dessert. No one could fail to notice Beth's mood. She looks tight-faced, controlling her anger, not speaking. There is a silence you could cut with a knife.

Annie glances over her shoulder towards the closed door of the living room where the phone is.

This door opens and JP enters. His mood has dramatically changed: now it's a defiant cheerfulness. He sits down in his place and with a flourish removes the saucepan lid which has been placed over his plate to keep it warm. He pretends to be ravished by the humble meal which is congealing underneath it. His merriment gets no response. Beth gives him a scorching look. Vicki polishes off her pudding without looking up, and Tim and Annie get up and leave the table as if for study. JP begins to eat his main course, ignoring the dirty looks he is getting.

After dinner, Vicki is watching TV. She hears muffled voices arguing in the kitchen, and glances apprehensively up towards the door.

In the kitchen Beth and JP are arguing, keeping their voices down. The kettle is boiling madly, unnoticed, filling the room with steam. Tea things stand ready on a tray.

JP (*fiercely*): And where is the leg *you* stand on? What lesson can *you* give of fidélité?

BETH: You told me it was finished.

JP: I thought it was.

BETH: We *agreed* it was.

JP: *You* agreed. *I* did not agree.

BETH: She's a dumb-cluck. A *twit*.

JP: She is young. I like her. She is full of life. And she is not always speaking about her *rights*.

BETH (*contemptuously*): She can't even pronounce your name.

JP (*furious*): And I can't pronounce yours. *Bef.*

He heads for the door. He is halfway into the dining room when she chucks the full sugar bowl at him. The bowl hits the door frame just above his head with a terrific crash. Sugar and broken china fly everywhere. Vicki sits up with a jerk.

JP barges across the living room, sugar in his hair and on his shoulders, walking fast, black-faced with rage, looking straight ahead. He strides out the front door which he violently slams behind him.

Vicki can see Beth in the doorway in the steam-filled kitchen, hands hanging down, shaking with fury.

―――――――――

Some hours later, Beth is lying on the bed reading. She has been crying. JP comes in with a cup of tea, puts it on the bedside table, and sits beside her.

BETH (*bleakly*): I smashed my best brown bowl.

JP: Why can't you be more reasonable. She is only—

BETH (*cuts across him*): I don't need you to *reason* with me. Put your arms around me. That's all I need.

JP does so, but stiffly, keeping his torso separate.

BETH (*on the verge of tears again*): I just want you to *love* me.

JP (*with a nervous laugh*): Oui—mais 'Pour être aimé, il faut être aimable'. (*Yes—but 'To be loved, one must be lovable'.*)

BETH (*twisting away from him, crying, angry*): Do you think I need to be *told* I'm not lovable? I *know* that! I know what I'm like! I'm bossy, impatient, too motherly, ill-mannered, unfaithful, greedy, a spend-thrift. (*She howls with abandon.*)

JP (*quietly*): C'est pas ça que je voulais dire. (*That's not what I meant.*)

Again, the possibility of connection between them has been missed. Beth lies there hopelessly bawling.

JP stands up. He sees the doona is all crooked; he picks it up (revealing Beth flat on her back in her nightie, arms by her sides) and repositions it over her—but he puts it on sideways without noticing, and her feet are sticking out. He kisses her cheek and tiptoes towards the door, eager to escape.

———

Down in the yard Vicki, one foot on the bottom stair, is calling out, loudly because of the background roar of racing cars from the TV in the living room.

VICKI: JP! The Grand Prix's started!

JP slides out of the bedroom door.

Beth lies there, still letting out the odd sob. Then she gets out of bed, turns the doona round the right way, and climbs back in. She turns off the light.

Next morning, Beth is on her hands and knees on the dining room floor, sweeping up the sugar with a dustpan and brush: humiliating evidence of her outburst. The phone rings in the living room, and is answered. Beth keeps working wretchedly, stiff-faced. Vicki enters.

VICKI: I got the job. Word-processing.

BETH (*mechanically, trying to smile*): Good on you.

VICKI: How long were *you* sending stuff out before *you* got published?

Beth doesn't answer. She keeps on sweeping.

VICKI: Hey. You know the arguments for and against abortion.

BETH: Yes.

VICKI: Well, could you just run through them for me one more time?

BETH (*taking a breath; still on her knees*): To have a baby, you have to really *want* one.

JP comes bustling in through the back door, on his way out to work. Beth stops talking and scrambles to her feet, in a hurry to go with him.

BETH (*urgently*): Wait for me!

Vicki is swept aside.

———————————

The same morning, in a café where people are having breakfast on their way to work, JP and Beth are sitting at a table near the window.

The waiter (tatts, gold chains, crim-style but friendly looking) pulls a cappuccino and slaps together a mortadella roll for an old dero in filthy black clothes and a greasy cap, and gestures to him to piss off.

The dero lurches out on to the pavement, where he can be seen for the whole of the scene, leaning against the plate glass, tearing at his roll with blackened teeth: a dark parody of the better-off breakfasters inside. Nobody pays him any attention.

The TV is on, on a high shelf in a corner: a blonde woman astrologer is giving the day's horoscopes. The waiter hops up on a chair to turn up the volume: the noise level in the café drops and everyone turns to listen to the soft, batty, whispering voice. JP alone continues to read the paper. Beth is just sitting there, unhappy and ignored.

BETH (*leaning towards JP*): We could try going out together more.

JP (*not taking his eyes off the paper*): And do what.

BETH: Have dinner or something? Isn't that what married people do?

She is not being ironic: she really doesn't know.

JP (*eyes on his paper*): And you see them sitting there, the woman desperately trying to make conversation, the man wishing he was somewhere else.

BETH: Well—but couldn't we at least try? (*Getting out her appointments diary.*) I don't have to do anything next Tuesday. Or Friday?

JP (*leans forward, speaks with bitter emphasis*): I don't want to be just *fitted in*.

Beth draws back. He returns to his paper.
    The power balance has shifted.

In the antiseptic corridor of a birth-control clinic, Vicki is walking along holding on to the arm of a young nurse. She is a bit groggy but clearly all right. They approach the waiting room which is down a flight of shallow stairs. As Vicki goes down with the nurse she can see Beth, who has not yet noticed her, sitting in a chair scribbling in her notebook.

VICKI (*relieved*): There she is.

NURSE: Your mum's come for you.

VICKI (*eagerly*): Beth!

Beth looks up. She shoves the notebook into her bag, and jumps up to dart forward and take over from the nurse.

Some minutes later.
    A taxi moves through the city streets.
    Beth and Vicki are sitting side by side in the back seat. Vicki looks upset and pale.

VICKI: They were so…fast.

BETH: I know. It's much more civilised than it was in my day.

VICKI: No—I mean in the interview, before…I thought they would have asked me a lot more questions.

BETH: What sort of questions?

VICKI: You know—who was responsible for me, and whether I'd thought properly about what I wanted to do.

BETH: They must have thought you were old enough and sensible enough to be responsible for yourself.

VICKI: When you did it, did you tell Mum?

BETH (*laughing, horrified*): Are you *kidding*?

VICKI: But who helped you?

BETH: Myself. My *self*.

VICKI (*getting trembly*): I think maybe people rushed me.

BETH: Hey. Come on. It's over now. Let's go home and I'll make you some chicken noodle soup. Out of a packet. Would you like that?

Vicki nods, sticking out her bottom lip childishly. Beth puts an arm around her shoulders.

BETH: You made the right decision, Vicki. I'm absolutely sure you did.

Vicki, however, is not so sure.

Saturday lunch at the house of Angelo and Sally. Beth and JP stand watching Angelo who is holding the new baby. He makes as if to pass it to JP; but JP puts out his palms in a gesture of reluctance.

JP: I'd drop him.

Beth rushes in eagerly and grabs the baby.

ANGELO: No you wouldn't. Hand him over, Beth.

BETH (*greedily*): In a minute. (*Sniffs at baby.*)

JP steps away to the window and looks out into the garden. Angelo stands beside him.

ANGELO: I got a couple of bags of chook manure and dug it in. Works wonders.

JP: Beans is what I like. At our other house, I would pick them up by the handfuls when I came home from work.

Beth is gooing over the baby.

JP: Now there is only concrete.

Half an hour later, the baby is asleep in its bassinet in the living room of Angelo and Sally's house. JP is standing beside the bassinet; he glances through the window out into the garden, where Angelo, Sally and Beth are sitting at the lunch table, unaware that he is watching them.

Out in the garden, at the table under the vines, Angelo is reproaching Beth.

ANGELO: You shouldn't have said that, Beth.

BETH: What?

ANGELO: All that ball-cutting stuff about why you married him.

BETH (*careless, defiant*): It's true. If he hadn't needed a passport we'd've just gone on living together. Anyway he was against marriage. On principle.

SALLY (*incredulously*): JP?

BETH (*getting defensive*): We *both* were. Listen—I had to buy my own *wedding* ring.

ANGELO (*not impressed*): Still. You shouldn't talk like that in front of people. It looks bad.

SALLY: It *hurts* him, Beth.

BETH (*crestfallen and ashamed*): I know. But I've never been any *good* at it. I don't even know how it's done. JP's the one who can do it.

ANGELO: What's 'it'?

BETH: Oh, *you* know—'sharing and caring'. Making plans. Being a couple. (She pulls a face, trying to make a joke of it.)

Angelo glances at Sally who drops her eyes in confusion. She is not sure which of them to support.

ANGELO: And what's so bad about that? What have you women *done* to yourselves? You're like husks.

Meanwhile, JP stands over the bassinet, studying the sleeping baby intently. He puts his face near the baby, sniffs at him, then with a glance behind him to make sure he's not being observed, he slips his hands under the tiny sausage roll of a body and lifts it out. He puts his hand carefully under the baby's head, holds him up against his chest, and murmurs to him in French.

A week later, on a Saturday morning, Beth comes rushing down the outside staircase, carrying a half-packed travel bag.

Vicki is hurrying along behind her, trying to keep up, trying to get Beth's attention.

VICKI: And Beth—Beth? You should *see* the people who come in there, and I have to type out their cases. A bloke that murdered his girlfriend's kid by running boiling water into the bath, and said it was an accident. Things that people ought to be *whipped* for. *Shot.*

BETH (*only half attending*): Crikey. I hope you're taking notes.

VICKI: But listen—I can't work out whether that's any worse than having an abortion.

Beth strides in the back door, across the dining room and into the living room, with Vicki close behind her. JP and Annie are playing a fast, noisy, fiercely competitive card game on the floor. Tim is watching them, laughing, strumming the ukulele. The radio is on—a dreary choir. There is a great racket in the room.

BETH: What? Of course it is. *Now*—

She dumps the bag on the couch and unzips it.

BETH: Do I need seven T-shirts? The traveller's rule: halve, and halve again.

She halves.

VICKI: I wish you weren't going.

BETH (*busy*): Phooey. You won't even notice I'm gone.

VICKI (*stubbornly*): Yes I will.

TIM (*wandering over*): Who'll look after Annie?

BETH (*teasing*): You will.

Tim looks alarmed and slightly guilty.

TIM: I'll never understand this family.

JP throws down the winning card, Annie howls with fury, JP cackles evilly and jumps to his feet, seizing the pile of cards.

JP (*loudly, merrily*): And who will look after *me*?

Beth looks at him, smiles, but does not answer. The awkwardness of their recent fights is still present.

JP approaches her; she is zipping up her suitcase. A little still moment between them.

JP (*mildly confrontational*): Why *are* you going out there? There's nothing there.

BETH (*softly, but straightening her back*): I might find something.

JP, shuffling the cards, turns away and speaks once more in his loud, jolly voice.

JP: You drag this poor old bastard out into the desert—

The door bell rings: three long, loud blasts. At the open door stands Father.

———————

Ten minutes later, Father's car pulls away. Tim, Annie, Vicki and JP stand on the front verandah looking at the empty street.

TIM (*to Annie*): Want to have a little play? Left hand right hand?

They run inside. Vicki and JP are left on the doorstep. JP stands aside for her to enter first. The piano starts up: Charlie Parker's bebop classic, 'Donna Lee', played badly, at a limping pace.

———————————

Next day.

Father's car goes barrelling down a country road. Beth is at the wheel. They are not conversing. They flash past a warning sign.

BETH: Border coming up. We'll have to get rid of all that fruit.

FATHER: I'm not chucking it out. What a waste. We could wrap it up and hide it under the bonnet.

BETH: I'd be too embarrassed.

FATHER (*surprised—isn't she supposed to be the bohemian?*): Would you?

BETH: What if there was an inspection? We'd look idiots, for a couple of oranges.

FATHER: We'll have to eat it, then. Pull over.

———————————

On the roadside moments later, within sight of the border fruit-fly inspection point, Beth and her father are standing beside the car, eating their way dutifully through a bag of oranges, bending over to let the juice drip down into the dust. They are guzzling and slurping, without pleasure: it is only to avoid detection or wastage.

Close-up of a mass of fresh fruit and vegetables from the market, arranged so as to tumble artistically out of a tilted basket on a table. We see Vicki, in the dining room at home, putting the finishing touches to her creation. African music is playing on the stereo.

JP enters the dining room from the kitchen, drying a spaghetti strainer with a tea towel.

VICKI (*standing back to admire*): Look! There's nothing more pleasing than a cornucopia.

She starts to dance to the music. She twirls merrily, skipping and bouncing, knees up, elbows pumping, her smiling face turned back to JP on a cheeky angle.

JP puts the spaghetti strainer on his head and falls into step beside her, keeping a sober expression. They move across the room and into the living room in unison, straight-faced, towards the front door, then break out of it with a laugh. High spirits: when the cat's away the mice can play.

JP peels off to sit down and read the Saturday papers, with the strainer still on his head, but Vicki keeps dancing by herself.

As she does so, her face becomes more thoughtful, and then sombre; but she keeps on dancing.

Father's car speeds across a hot, dry landscape. Beth is driving.

Father is trying to open a packet of CC's for her and is making heavy weather of it. He can't find the right angle on which to tear the cellophane. It is not a problem of physical weakness—he is strong and agile—but of not knowing the way things are done in the modern world. He is annoyed and embarrassed.

Beth grabs it from him and tears it open with her teeth, keeping her eyes on the road. She offers him one but his pride is hurt; he shakes his head and turns to look out the window. She starts to crunch them.

———————————

Beth is driving. The landscape now is practically a desert.

Father consults a map. They flash past a sign. He cranes his neck but can't get a proper look at it. Gives Beth a cross glance, which she does not notice.

BETH: What's the time?

FATHER: One-fifteen.

BETH: One-fifteen?

FATHER: I'm not changing it. I'm keeping it on Eastern Standard.

———————————

The car is now in red desert proper.

Beth slows down as they approach a tourist bus which has stopped by the roadside.

FATHER: What are you doing?

Beth doesn't answer.

FATHER: Why have you stopped here? Looks the same as everywhere else.

They pull up and get out.

A crowd of old people from the bus tour (most of them women) are taking photographs of the nothingness.

OLD MAN: (*to Father*): You can waste a lot of money taking photos. Unless you've got something like your wife on the side of the picture. A personal touch. Otherwise you're better off buying one of those folders with the views hanging off it.

FATHER: This is my daughter. Would she do?

The old man gives him a puzzled look.

———————

The car rolls on, with Beth at the wheel.

FATHER (*with contempt*): 'A personal touch'. Stupid old bugger. I'd much rather a plain landscape, wouldn't you? With no people in it?

BETH (*eager to talk about something*): I like interiors. Photos of things on tables.

FATHER (*losing interest as soon as she gets arty*): Can't see the interest of that. (*Looks out the window.*)
    Not many kangaroos. I thought we'd have seen herds and herds. No emus either. What's happened to this country?

We see the empty horizon passing.

––––––––––––––––

The empty horizon becomes a postcard. Pull back to show it is held in the chubby fingers of JP, who is examining it with dismayed fascination.

JP (*to himself, with feeling*): Quel pays affreux. It is all the same. C'est un pays perdu. Qu'est-ce que je fous ici? (*What a dreadful country. It's a* lost *country. What the hell am I doing here?*)

Behind him, boppy music. Tim, Vicki and Annie are mucking about in dress-ups, running to and fro. Vicki is putting on a Dolly Parton wig.

JP's gaze settles on Vicki as she arranges the wig on her head; her face, unaware of his scrutiny, is trembling with suppressed laughter at her part in the game.

———————————

Beth and her father have got out of the car and are standing separately, at some distance from the car, in featureless red country. Car ticks as it cools. They are bewildered, overwhelmed by the hugeness around them.

Father holds a map but his hand is dangling as if he had given up trying to navigate; the map no longer applies. Night is coming on. Colours very deep and spectacular.

———————————

Days later. Afternoon in the house.

At the table are Vicki, JP, Tim and Annie. They are all colouring in. A big box of pencils is open between them. Behind them the room is in disorder: pizza boxes, papers, etc., strewn all over the floor and furniture, empty stubbies on their sides, dirty dishes in piles.

But in spite of the disorder, the house is peaceful and slow because Beth is away.

There are many pauses in the talk. During silences, the sound of pencils moving against paper. Someone shows their work, others glance up, then it is quiet again.

In the corner the TV is on with no sound: a marathon,

runners slogging desperately along rainy roads; the pathos of this—their grim struggle contrasts with the voices of the cheerful colourers-in.

TIM: Did you get homesick when you were overseas, Vicki?

VICKI: Sometimes.

Pause.

VICKI: JP's overseas all the time, aren't you, JP.

They all look up at him, struck by this remark. They are in an agreeable, half-stunned state.

JP looks up too, sees that he has their attention fully; he gives a shy smile, not his usual clever one. They continue to colour in.

JP: There is one thing I miss. Andouillettes.

VICKI: What's that?

JP: A kind of sausage.

Pause. Colouring in.

VICKI: I thought about you, JP, one time when I was in Italy.

JP (*flirtatiously*): Only one time?

VICKI (*smiling; looking at her work*): Some people took me to their place by the sea. They were really nice people but they used to laugh whenever I spoke. I had to put up with it because they were my friends. Anyway I went out on this balcony and looked down on the beach, and it was disgusting. It was narrow and made out of stones, and there was *matter* floating in the water—oil and plastic milk bottles and stuff. I couldn't help it—I started to bawl. I wanted to yell at them, 'Okay! I'm only an Australian and I make stupid mistakes when I talk and my clothes are all wrong and you can laugh at me if you like, but at least I know what a proper *beach* looks like'.

Pause. Everyone listening as they colour.

VICKI: One with *waves*.

TIM: Don't they have waves over there?

JP: What has this to do with me?

VICKI: I was ashamed of how mean Beth and I used to be when you played your daggy French rock records.

JP picks up Vicki's hand and formally kisses it.

ANNIE (*glancing up and down, colouring even more vigorously*): Ewww, *yuck*.

It is a hot night. Beth and her father come out of the motel dining room to the yard between the rooms. It is clear from their demeanour that they have nothing much to say to each other, are bored with each other's company through the long driving day, and are now parting for the evening to go to their rooms. They walk together to a certain point in the carpark, then peel off and head for their separate doors.

Ten minutes later, Father comes out of his room. The screen door bangs shut behind him. He walks across the gravel yard, carrying a heavy jerry can. He approaches Beth's door: he can see a light on behind the screen. He knocks. She comes to the door, holding a book.

FATHER (*gruffly*): Want some tank water from home? To have in your room overnight?

BETH (*without interest, oblivious to the meaning of the gesture*): Oh…no thanks. I never get thirsty at night.

He nods and turns away. He is hurt, but remains impassive. Beth's door closes. He trudges away with his jerry can, head down.

Back at the house, late on a hot afternoon, Annie and Vicki are messing round with Beth's things, both in a state of busy, intense personal concentration. Each is lost in her own fantasy at first, though they communicate in a two-level exchange.

Vicki behaves in this scene as if Beth were her mother. The clothes they try on are ones we have never seen Beth wearing: linen suit, high heels, dresses with big full skirts. They are playing in Beth's discarded fantasies of herself.

VICKI: But do you think they still love each other?

ANNIE (*with unintentionally comic dignity*): How would I know? I've got my own life to live.

VICKI: That colour definitely doesn't suit you.

Vicki fossicks on Beth's desk among her papers.

VICKI: Ooh, look. She's trying to write a play. Or a movie. Listen. 'Her shoes looked like two crows' beaks.' Hey! *I* said that!

ANNIE: She writes down everything. (*Holds up a complicated bra.*) What's this thing?

VICKI: What if she wrote a movie about us. Would you go in it?

ANNIE: Don't *snoop*, Vicki. My God—flares.

VICKI (*lifting pillow*): Where's her diary.

Annie slams the pillow back down but Vicki picks up Beth's nightie and smells it.

VICKI: Mmmm. Smell this. Like when you were a baby.

ANNIE (*putting on jewellery*): I don't remember.

VICKI: I do.

ANNIE (*looking at herself in the mirror*): Was I cute?

VICKI (*moving to the smaller mirror on the dressing table*): I only saw you in the distance. I had to wait in the car outside your house with Dad. He wouldn't let me go in.

ANNIE (*still at the long mirror; astonished*): Why not?

VICKI (*at the small mirror; speaking casually*): Oh, he couldn't stand your father. *Any* bloke Beth brought home he couldn't stand. He wouldn't go to her wedding or anything. He was *jealous* of your father.

Annie listens, stock still in items of her mother's clothing and jewellery.

VICKI: When you were born he wouldn't go to the hospital to see you. He even tried to stop Mum from going.

Annie makes no reply; she is rather shocked.

VICKI: Hasn't she ever told you all this?

ANNIE: No.

VICKI: You ask her one day.

Annie in Beth's big dress goes to the window in silence and looks out.

VICKI: Are you upset?

ANNIE (*lying*): No.

VICKI: I wonder how they're getting on out there.

We can see the hand of cypress trees, which Annie too is looking at from her position at the window. Against the remaining light in the sky, they look very dark. The rest of the dialogue is in voice-over.

VICKI: She's probably murdered him by now.

ANNIE: Maybe he deserves it.

VICKI: And buried him in a shallow grave.

ANNIE: Shutup, Vicki. You're giving me the creeps.

Night, in a desert motel.

Beth looks up from the notebook she is scribbling in, and sees on TV a show about doctors and patients—a documentary. A woman is having a caesarean: her abdomen is slit open with a scalpel and a baby pops out into the surgeon's gloved hands. Beth gives a gasp and watches intently.

Vicki, on the couch in front of the TV at home, sees the same thing and bursts into tears.

Father, ensconced in glory in his motel bed with an open wine bottle, the esky beside him, a newspaper folded tightly into the square of the crossword, his pencil nicely sharpened, glances up and sees the same thing on TV. He gets out of bed and with distaste flips the channel over to the cricket.

JP enters the living room carrying two bowls of soup, and heads for the couch where Vicki is sitting, bent over herself, weeping helplessly. On the screen we see the baby being dealt with: tubes are thrust down its nose, a little silver paper cap is put on its head to keep it warm, its tiny arms wave feebly in protest.

JP, shocked by Vicki's weeping, puts down the soup and opens his arms to her.

JP (*softly*): Mais qu'est-ce qu'il y a? Qu'est-ce qui se passe? (*What's the matter? What's going on?*)

Vicki can't explain. He rocks her, murmurs in French. She lets herself be comforted.

———————————

In the motel, Beth with full attention watches the baby being dealt with. She too is moved, on the verge of tears.

———————————

On the living-room sofa, Vicki and JP eat their soup. Vicki is still taking big quivering breaths.

JP: You should have asked *me*. Beth—with her everything must be cleared up always. She can't wait.

VICKI: I never thought you'd be interested.

JP: You could have given *me* this baby.

VICKI: Oh, don't tease me, JP.

JP: You always think I am tizzing.

She stops slurping her soup and stares at him.

He leans forward and kisses her on the mouth. The phone rings. They take no notice. It keeps ringing.

JP and Vicki are staring at each other, breathless.

———————

Beth is standing in a phone box on a desert road near the motel. It is totally black outside.

A lit road-train goes past. A stack of coins stands on the top of the phone. We hear it ring and ring. Nobody answers.

Finally Beth puts down the receiver. An avalanche of coins falls into the return chute.

———————

Father's car is raising dust on an unmade road. It is a hot morning.

Beth is driving. A cow appears, looking very small, on the verge of the road a hundred yards ahead of the car.

FATHER: Ease 'er down.

No reaction from Beth.

FATHER (*with more authority*): *Ease 'er down.*

Beth does not respond. He looks sharply at her.

FATHER (*bellowing*): I said EASE 'ER DOWN!!!

Beth, offended, pulls over, stops the car, pulls on the hand-brake rather hard. They are still yards away from the animal: there was no danger of their hitting it.

Father leans across and lets the hand-brake off again.

BETH: *Why'd you do that?*

FATHER (*faking reasonableness*): That's no way to put on a hand-brake.

BETH (*with exaggerated restraint*): Dad. I have been driving now for *over twenty years*. In that time I have *never had an accident*. I *know* how to put on a hand-brake.

FATHER: You *yanked* it. Maybe in the kind of bombs *you* drive that's how you put a hand-brake on.

This is their customary mode of behaviour with each other. They resemble each other; thus, any minor incident, a certain tone of voice, a momentary dinting of their vanity can trigger off ancient, unconscious, unresolved hostilities.

Beth puts the car in gear and drives back on to the road. Grim silence.

They approach a petrol station, a dismal dump on the endless plain. Beth is still at the wheel.

FATHER: Turn in here.

Beth obeys, and lines the back of the car up with the pump as if for a fill.

FATHER (*irritably*): Back up, will you? I only want to compare prices.

BETH (*savagely*): I can't read your mind.

She gets out, slams the door loudly, marches away towards the roadhouse.

Father gets out of the car, walks around it and gets into the driving seat. Beth comes out of the cafe unwrapping a sandwich and starting to eat it. She gets into the passenger seat. They do not look at each other. He drives away.

FATHER: It's a wonder you don't get fat, the amount you eat between meals.

BETH: *You* should talk.

FATHER: What's biting *you*?

BETH: I think we should talk about it.

FATHER: About what?

BETH: About why we have these stupid fights!

FATHER: You start them. Doing stupid things. Slamming car doors. Yanking the hand-brake like that.

BETH (*starting to cry, stuffing the sandwich in*): I'm over forty. This is undignified.

FATHER (*turning away, embarrassed*): Gawd, Beth—you get so flamin' worked up about everything!

BETH: I hate the way we fight. I don't want to be like this with you. I thought if we came away out here where there was nobody else we might be able to—to—

She is sobbing and swallowing bites of the sandwich; she can't speak.

FATHER (*completely baffled*): Able to *what*?

BETH: To *stop*. We've been fighting like this ever since I was fifteen. It's ruining my life. I don't even know what we're fighting *about*.

FATHER (*irritated*): If you didn't act like an idiot, the way you do, there'd be no *need* for us to fight.

BETH (*hopelessly trying to get herself under control*): It can't be all my fault. Why is it all my fault? Is it because I'm the oldest? Is that why you've always been tougher on me?

FATHER (*disgusted*): I can't see any point in thrashing round 'talking things through'. Everybody makes mistakes, but Gawd! You're as bad as your mother. *She* always wants to talk about things. What's there to say? Everybody *talks* too much.

BETH (*starting to cry again*): But you're my father. And I love you.

He looks round sharply at her, astonished, then away again, deeply appalled and embarrassed.

BETH: And we're both too *old* to be fighting like this.

Beth finishes the sandwich and screws up the paper bag fiercely, holding it in her fist and keeping her eyes on the road outside the side window.

Father keeps driving, eyes straight ahead.

———————————

Father is now at the wheel. They arrive at a gorge.

A big flash new 4WD is parked under a tree, with a large new caravan attached, but no one is in sight.

Beth and Father get out and walk along the stony gorge (he's in front, she follows) to a large pool of water. By the water's edge there are four pairs of thongs left in a neat row.

BETH (*gloomily*): Look. The suicide of the family.

84

They stand by the water.

Beth picks up a stone and tries to skim it. It sinks. Father skims his beautifully.

FATHER (*trying to be conciliatory; joking his way out of it, as he has always done before*): That pool will eventually be filled right up, with the stones that people chuck into it, trying to skim.

BETH (*unfriendly*): Hardly.

FATHER: You don't think so? Not in a thousand years?

He is trying to tease her out of her miserable mood, but she won't bite.

BETH (*bitterly*): The human race won't *be* here in a thousand years.

———————

Teatime, at a primitive motel. Beth and her father are sitting there dully, having finished their main course. It is still light outside.

There is no one else in the room.

The door to the kitchen is open and through it comes the cheerful noise of someone washing up and whistling, a radio, the clash of plates.

A waitress comes out with a sundae dish and puts it in front of Beth.

BETH: I thought I said only one scoop.

WAITRESS (*merrily*): It looked a bit lonely, all by itself, so I thought, well—

She gestures with both hands outspread, then bounces away. Beth looks sombrely at the large sundae.

FATHER: Hey.

Beth looks up.

FATHER: I'll give you a hand.

She passes him the spoon and he begins to eat, but with scrupulous and flamboyant daintiness he keeps to his side of the dish and demolishes only one of the scoops.

Beth can't help grinning. She tries to cover her mouth with her hand.

Father looks at her with false soberness, chewing.

It is a warm evening, back in the city.

In the lane outside the back gate, Tim is waiting with his bike. Annie comes out, eager and flustered.

TIM: Cute beret. It's got little holes for your antennae to poke through.

ANNIE (*flattered*): It's Mum's.

She hops on the bar and they wheel away.

———————————

Night now, in the desert. The sky is white with stars.
A deep silence.
    Beth and her father walk along a dirt road.

FATHER: This is far enough.

BETH: No, come on—let's see if we can get away from the
    lights.

FATHER: Where *is* everyone?

BETH: They're inside watching *The Texas Chainsaw
    Massacre* on video.

He laughs. They walk.

BETH: Hey, Dad. Have you ever—

FATHER: What?

BETH: Doesn't matter.

They walk.

BETH: Hey, Dad. Do you believe in God?

FATHER (*taken aback*): What?

BETH: God. Do you believe there is one?

FATHER: Me? Do *I*?

BETH: Yeah.

They walk on.

BETH: Well—do you?

FATHER (*sighs*): Ah, no…When I was a kid and they told me that God made everything, I used to rack m' brains tryin' to nut out who made God.

Beth laughs.

FATHER: *Does* anyone know that? Has anyone ever nutted that one out? Everyone's got a theory, but…

They walk. Beth is looking at him expectantly: she is hoping for an answer.

FATHER: Mum and I went on a tour once, down the Danube. We got off at some famous old city or other, I forget, mighta been Budapest. They dragged us into a cathedral. Oh, huge, it was. I got sick of the guide telling us what this was and what that was, so I sat down on a bench under a colossal dome. There was another bloke sitting near me. He looked at me and he said, 'What do *you* think?' I said, 'Whaddya mean, what do I think?' He said, 'What do you think about God?' I said, 'I'm not convinced. What do *you* think?' And he said, 'Nothing. Nothing at all.'

A pause. They walk.

BETH: There is no God?

FATHER: There is no God. He said, 'Look. I'm a Jew. I got out of Germany b' the skin o' m' teeth. My entire family was exterminated. How could I think anything else?' And I agree. What *I* reckon is—if there's a God, why didn't he come down and stop Hitler? Why didn't he come down and stop the death camps, and the Nazis?

They walk. A pause. Father is out of breath, unused to extended speech.

BETH: And what about dying?

FATHER (*wary*): What about it?

BETH: Are you afraid of it?

Father gives an odd smile and a shrug, looking down at his feet as they walk.

Long silence.

BETH: *Are* you?

FATHER (*at last*): Fair go.

Still walking, not looking at him, Beth takes his arm, an action so unprecedented between them that he almost jumps before accepting it, and can't look at her.

They walk, arm in arm. The sky is absolutely swimming with stars. The silence is tremendous.

A great gush of water, a noisy fountain in a city park.

Towards it are riding Tim and Annie on the bike; she is crouching in the curve of his body.

The fountain is *shouting*.

They don't speak. Their faces are calm, absorbed.

Towards midnight, the same night. Vicki is asleep in her room. Outside the window there are sounds of metal on metal, thumps, rattling.

Vicki stumbles, half asleep, to look out.

JP's car is parked right outside. In the dark Vicki can make out a figure—there is a man in the car. Now she sees him crouching to hot-wire it. The motor roars, stalls, roars again. Vicki bangs her fist hard on the window. He looks up.

Vicki is standing in her nightie, arms folded, staring in at him with a stupefied expression of outrage.

THIEF (*winds down window: drunk, agitated—as if annoyed at being interrupted in urgent business*): I've gotta go after them! I've gotta get to Cronulla!

VICKI: What! What are you doing?

THIEF: M' girl! She went off with m' mate!

VICKI: But this is *our* car!

THIEF (*suddenly deflated, like someone woken from a dream*): Oh Jesus...Sorry. Look, I'm sorry.

He gets out of the car and stumbles away up the street, mumbling to himself.

———————

In his room at the back of the house, upstairs, JP hears nothing of all this: he is asleep. He wakes as the door opens: he sees a woman standing against the dim light from the hallway. Sound of her breathing hard, from having run up the stairs.

JP (*thinking it's Beth*): C'est toi? Tu es rentrée? Qu'est-ce que tu fais là? (*Is it you? Are you back? What are you doing here?*)

VICKI: Someone was stealing your car.

She walks in and stands next to the bed.

He sits up, fully awake. A charged moment. Vicki is panting.

He puts out one hand and takes hold of her by the wrist.

She puts one knee on the bed.

Very late that night, the back gate opens and Tim and Annie creep in. Tim is wheeling his bike. At the bottom of the stairs they kiss, very hesitantly: the first time. They are smiling.

ANNIE: Good night!

TIM: Good night!

Annie dashes up the back stairs, being careful to make no noise.

In bed, Vicki is falling asleep in JP's arms.

We see his face: calm, almost smiling. He is guarding her. She is someone who needs to be looked after, who needs him.

JP (*murmuring, to put her to sleep*): I can wait. There is no hurry. We can work it out.

Vicki's nightie is on the floor beside the bed.

———————————

It's dawn. The sky is pink. Birds are singing loudly.

Vicki, in her hastily donned nightie, comes creeping down the outside stairs towards the back door.

———————————

Ten days later, at five in the afternoon, Father's car, red with dust, pulls away from the kerb, outside Beth's house.

Beth carrying her bag, approaches the front door. The house looks attractive.

The window and door open; somebody is playing the piano.

Beth stops at the front door. Tim and Annie are playing the piano left hand right hand, 'Donna Lee'—playing it now with more skill, speed and panache than when Beth left, though it is still much too sophisticated and difficult for them.

The room is a pigsty.

As Beth stands in the doorway, they bring the tune to a triumphant conclusion, with a flourish and almost in time except that Annie is half a beat behind.

ANNIE (*throwing her hands in the air like a virtuoso*): Yay!!!

She looks up and sees Beth standing there.

ANNIE (*hopping up to kiss her*): Mum! Hi! Did you hear us?

BETH (*hugging her*): Beautiful. Well—what's been happening? Did I miss anything?

TIM (*helpfully*): There's a Jelly Roll Morton revival—among *my* friends, anyway.

BETH: Where are the others?

ANNIE: I don't know—out—working, maybe.

They stand awkwardly. Tim picks up the ukulele, runs off a riff.

BETH: Did you miss me?

ANNIE: Well—I *have* been pretty busy.

BETH (*to tease*): You could at least *say* you missed me.

ANNIE: Oh Mu-um!

They laugh, and look away from each other.

Ten minutes later up the street comes Vicki, bouncing along, keen to be home. She sees JP backing down the front steps of the house, and gives a little hop. He is holding a paper bag with two stubbies in it. She skips up to him.

JP (*quietly*): She is back.

VICKI (*wind out of her sails*): We haven't cleaned up.

JP: It is too late now.

VICKI: I might go round the block.

She walks away, head down.
    JP continues to dither, nerving himself to go in.
    Meanwhile, we can faintly hear Beth's voice somewhere inside the house, telling a great tale of travel.

BETH: No sooner do we get the car back on the road then he notices he's lost his watch. Total panic: 'I got it in Geneva—we'll have to go back.' Big U-turn into the valley, which consists entirely of sand and stones. All these Aborigines are standing round under a tree. We pull up near them and start to get out; but before my father can open his mouth, one of the black blokes steps forward, holding out the watch, and says, 'Is this what you're looking for?'

In the kitchen, Beth is already vigorously mopping the kitchen floor, which is partly covered with sheets of newspaper. Tim is sitting up on the bench with his feet out of the way, strumming the ukulele softly and fast. *He* is chattering now.

TIM: ...he was playing these very...esoteric chords. They could have been in any key whatsoever. We clapped them out of pity. I don't know what it is that makes one band more successful than another, and I'm sick of thinking about it.
   Hi, JP.

JP picks his way towards Beth, leans forward off an island of newspaper, kisses her on the cheek.

JP: Ça c'est bien passé? (*Did it go well?*)

BETH: Oui.

She is glad to see him but cross that he has let the house get into such a state.

JP opens the bag of stubbies, takes them out, opens one and hands it to her. Tim fades out into the dining room.

JP: Alors—c'est mission accomplished? With your papa it is now like this? (*Holds up two crossed fingers.*)

His tone is lightly teasing, apparently affectionate, but something in it makes her uncomfortable. She bristles slightly.

BETH (*still holding the mop*): Can I have mine in a glass? Please?

JP pauses for a fraction of a second before opening the cupboard. Customs have changed in her absence.

Vicki comes in from the lane in a resolute rush.

BETH (*gladly*): Hullo!

VICKI: Gee, you're brown!

They hug heartily. JP looks on.

———————

That night, Beth and JP are lying on their backs in bed, awake, talking.

JP (*with an incredulous laugh*): You asked him this? Was he embarrassed?

BETH: Not half as embarrassed as you.

They both laugh.
    Pause.

JP: If I was religious, I would choose Islam. Then I could have two wives.

BETH (*trying to go along with his joke*): Two wives. (*Laughs uncertainly.*) Where would that leave *me*?

JP: See? You turn everything to yourself, straight away. (*As if preparing to drop the subject:*) It's nothing. I think about it when I'm stuck in the traffic.

BETH: Got anyone special in mind?

JP: Who? *Who* would I have in mind?

Pause. Beth is thinking.

BETH: That's hippie stuff. It never worked.

JP: But for me, having to choose is not natural.

BETH: Why?

JP (*as if thinking out loud*): For me to leave you would be cruel.

BETH (*with a little flare of pride*): Cruel? To me?

JP: Non! To *me*! I am not thinking of you, at this moment!

Pause.

JP: But if I had another wife, then I could love *you* better.

BETH (*touched and relieved*): So you *do* still love me, then.

JP (*hastily, brushing it aside*): Of course.

Pause. They lie there quietly.

JP (*lightly*): Why *don't* you become a Christian? Or a Buddhist? Then you could forgive me for everything I do.

Beth gives a puzzled laugh.

JP: Let's go to sleep now.

BETH: All right.

JP kisses her cheek.

BETH: Your skin's cold.

They settle themselves for sleep.

Next morning. Beth is standing just inside the back gate, drinking a glass of orange juice. She notices something in the back seat of an old Morris parked in the lane outside the gate: somebody is asleep in there, under a leather jacket. Tim comes rushing out the back door, heading for university.

BETH: Hey. (*Gestures towards the sleeping person.*) There's a body in there.

TIM (*slightly embarrassed*): That's Spenny.

BETH: Who?

TIM (*speaks in low, confidential voice*): I *said* to him, look, Spenny, if you feel funny about sleeping top to toe with me in my bed, there's heaps of other blankets and stuff out in the shed—but he said no, he absolutely wanted to sleep in his new car. So I said, you've hurt me, Spenny— but he insisted.

He sets out up the street.
    Annie rushes out with her satchel.

BETH: Hey. Who's Spenny?

ANNIE: That's him in there.

Beth stands with her glass as Annie darts away to school. Another life in the house has begun, one which she has not initiated and does not control.

She looks at the distant row of cypress trees. They are dark, even in morning sunshine, and quite still, like a hand held up to say Stop or even Help.

Later the same morning, in the dining room, Vicki is making herself a bag of lunch, throwing it together in a hurry. Beth is cleaning her boots.

VICKI: And did he climb it?

BETH: He didn't even get out of the car.

They laugh.

BETH: So—how were things while I was away?

VICKI (*very small pause*): Good. Same as usual. Plenty of laughs.

BETH: And what about Tim and Annie.

VICKI (*pushes down her sock to show Beth her ankle*): Look at this scab. I must have scratched it on something.

BETH: Vicki? What about Tim and Annie?

VICKI (*vaguely*): They seem fine.

BETH: Yes, but are they—you know—

VICKI (*irritated*): Oh, leave them alone, Beth, can't you? It's none of your business.

BETH (*bores on*): I just hope she won't do something stupid like fall in love and fail her exams.

VICKI: What if she does? Love is more important than honours. Love's more important than *anything*.

JP comes bustling through the dining room on his way out to work. Vicki drops her eyes but Beth pursues him with her questions, pestering; we feel her *anxiety*.

BETH: Where will I meet you, JP? Or will you pick me up? I'll be—

JP (*irritably*): Non! Take the bus and I will see you outside.

He charges off out the front door. Beth stands still. Vicki is busying herself, eyes down.

———————————

Late the same morning, when everyone else has left the house, Beth stands in the middle of her sister's room, not doing anything or looking at anything; just standing there. *She* doesn't know, either, why she is there.

Her expression is confused. Instinct is working, but it hasn't broken through yet to consciousness.

Three faces in a row: Vicki, JP and Beth. Their different expressions: Vicki contained, eyes down; JP having trouble concealing amazement, dismay and scorn; Beth ashamed and keeping an eye on JP's reaction. Voice-over of Mayor leading, with other voices droning along behind, in a perfunctory manner.

MAYOR: I swear by almighty God—that I will be faithful — and bear true allegiance...

Pull back to show that the three are standing just inside the door of the chamber where a naturalisation ceremony is already in progress: JP is late. The Mayor and Co. are all kitted up, on a dais. New citizens stand in a row at the front, friends and guests seated behind them on folding chairs. The new citizens are being sworn in, in groups of four at a time.

In the background, an awful attempt at a festive setting: trestle tables, urns, massed ranks of cups and saucers, plates of sweet biscuits, big jugs of cordial. No wine or beer.

Beth is holding a bunch of small red roses. She offers one to JP.

JP: Non! This is nothing special for me. It's just a piece of paper.

He hurries away towards his rightful place in the new citizens' row.

BETH (*desperately, to Vicki*): It's a time warp. It's still the fifties in here.

Vicki makes no response: Beth cannot spark a laugh out of her.

The dreary ceremony continues.

When it's over, JP stands holding his scroll and looking cross and embarrassed.

Beth puts out her hand to shake his, protecting herself by making a joke out of it. He takes her hand and presents his cheeks for her to kiss.

BETH: Congratulations.

They stand about, with Vicki, silent, uncomfortable, not knowing where to look.

BETH (*awkwardly*): Okay—I'm going to get some food for dinner. Will you both be home? Because I've invited Sal and Angelo, to sort of celebrate.

JP (*trying to be light*): There is something to celebrate?

BETH (*battling on*): Well—I'm back. And you're an Australian now.

She goes off, carrying her flowers. They stand and watch her go; then they exchange a frightened, passionate look.

———————————

Early that evening, in the dining room, Beth is dumping a folded cloth and some cutlery on the table when Vicki and JP come in from the front door. Their faces are open and soft.

BETH (*trying not to sound reproachful*): I was wondering where you two had got to!

VICKI: We saw a movie.

BETH: Oh! Was it in black and white, or colour?

JP (*snaps, like an adolescent at his mother*): Colour, of course.

BETH (*hurt*): Why do you answer me like that?

JP (*his irritation out of control*): Because it is a stupid question. Films are all made in colour now. How could it have been in black and white? Why do you ask this question?

BETH (*baffled and wounded*): *Manhattan* was in black and white, wasn't it?

JP: You don't even want to know! You just ask questions to have something to say! You must always have something to say!

He marches out the back door and into the yard, to go upstairs. Beth at the table is silent with humiliation. Vicki can hardly bear to look at her.

VICKI (*in a low voice*): How can you let him speak to you like that?

———————————

Meanwhile, Angelo and Sally, dressed up to dine out, are sitting at the backyard table having a drink. They are not visible from the dining room but have heard the exchange between JP and Beth and are now sitting bright-faced with embarrassment. The baby is on the ground, in a basket.

106

JP, surging out the back door on his way to the stairs, comes upon them without expecting to. He has forgotten they were coming; he jams on the brakes and shifts into sociable gear. He shakes Angelo's hand and kisses Sally.

Vicki slides through the yard behind him, nodding and waving to the guests; she runs up the stairs and disappears.

SALLY: Congratulations, JP.

ANGELO: Where's your certificate, mate?

JP (*airily, to get a laugh*): I put it in the bin.

JP pours himself a glass of wine and pulls out a chair for himself, but Beth comes to the kitchen door with a big saucepan, about to carry it into the dining room.

BETH: This is ready, Jean-Pierre. Can you call the others, please?

JP puts down his glass and moves towards the stairs.
Angelo and Sally stand too.

On the upstairs verandah, out of sight of the guests, JP is holding Vicki in his arms. He is ardent, and urgent; but she is standing still in his embrace, frightened, with her arms hanging down and her head on one side.

JP (*whispering, as if answering her doubts*): I am *ready* for a scandal.

The end of the meal on the same evening. At the table in the dining room are Beth, JP, Vicki, Annie, Tim, Angelo, Sally.

Sally is working hard, being charming to the kids who are chattering with her, unaware of the undercurrents of tension at the table. JP and Vicki are quiet. Beth is trying to cover up by being hostly; Angelo has smelt a rat and keeps looking from face to face.

SALLY: I used to work in an old people's home, when I was a student.

ANNIE: Did they get many visitors?

SALLY: Not really. They were pretty out of it, most of them.

ANNIE: I think that's *awful*.

TIM: I'd *never* put *my* mum away. (*To Annie:*) Would you?

Annie turns straight to Beth and launches into the Butterworth game.

ANNIE: As soon as you've finished your dinner, Cheryl, we'll be taking you back to Braemar Lodge.

BETH (*falling in with the game*): I'm not going back there. I don't want to.

ANNIE (*sweetly persuasive, but with menace*): Don't be silly, Cheryl. You love it there. Matron's a very nice lady.

BETH (*sullenly*): I hate Matron.

ANNIE (*carolling*): But Matron's *nice*! She lets you watch 'Perfect Match' with all the other ladies—doesn't she, Chantelle?

Annie tries to hook Vicki to play her usual part in the game, but Vicki won't bite; keeps her eyes away, with an embarrassed look.

BETH: No. I'm not going back. This is where I belong. I won't go.

TIM (*in stage whisper*): Want me to go for a syringe?

ANNIE: Not yet. Leave it to me. She trusts me. (*Aloud:*) Now come on Cheryl. Don't make a fuss. I'll get your cardy. Jason's going to drive you back to Braemar now, aren't you Jason? (*to JP*)

JP and Vicki have their eyes on their plates. Sally can't help laughing but Angelo is frankly appalled.

JP: Arrête, arrête, Annie—not these 'orrible Butterworths.

ANGELO: Who the hell are the Butterworths?

ANNIE (*cheerful, bright, oblivious*): Oh, they're a family of a mother and two daughters. The mother's an old moll, and the daughters are lazy, stupid and mean.

ANGELO (*laughing in horror*): You lot are sick.

Small pause.

BETH (*abashed*): Sometimes we do Chekhov.

Sally laughs again.

JP: It is a game of anti-working class.

BETH (*serious and tired*): No, it's not. It's not anti-anything. I wish I was like Cheryl. Cheryl's better than me. She's rough as bags, but she's got more heart.

Everyone looks at her, surprised. She has quietly dropped her bundle.

Later the same night, Beth is alone on the upstairs verandah in the dark, sitting on the bench.

JP comes up the stairs looking for her.

She looks round with a hurt expression, but glad to see

him and trying to smile, hoping perhaps that he has come to say he is sorry, to *fix* everything. But he looks tense, overwrought, even scared.

JP: We didn't know where you were.

Beth just looks at him, waiting.

JP: I'm going to bed.

BETH: Tu m'embrasses pas? (*Aren't you going to kiss me?*)

She means a goodnight kiss.

JP (*blurting it out*): There is something between me and Vicki.

Beth, shocked, laughs.

JP: It's serious.

Beth gets up and blunders past him, in towards the bathroom, looking back over her shoulder at him as she walks away, laughing foolishly.

———————

Beth is standing in the bathroom in her nightie, stunned, not moving.

Propped on top of the cupboard, wrinkled from steam, are several photos, including one of Beth and Vicki.

Beth picks up a lump of curtain rod that is leaning against the wall and lays about her in the bathroom, smashing the photos, a vase, a couple of jars, sending shampoo bottles flying. She hits about wildly, with violence.

Vicki is standing in the middle of her bedroom as if waiting for something. She hears the explosion of breakage from another room, and puts her hands over her face, flinching with raised shoulders.

Beth is sitting on the edge of the bath.

JP opens the door. He is fearful; but he crunches through the wreckage and sits beside her on the bath. For a moment they're silent.

JP: Are you angry with me? Are you jealous?

BETH: What I am feeling makes jealousy seem like a surface tremor.

JP: Why don't you cry?

BETH: I will. Later.

Sound of front door slamming sharply downstairs. JP jumps.

BETH (*with mockery*): Aren't you going with your lover?

JP: No.

Pause.

BETH (*dully*): *Do* you love her?

JP (*quietly and humbly*): It is as if, before I did not know what love was.

Pause.

BETH (*bitterly*): And what *is* love.

JP (*quietly*): Don't mock me.

BETH: I think I must be a very unbearable person.

JP begins quietly to cry. He leans sideways until his head is resting on her shoulder. Slowly, wearily, she puts her arm around him.

———————

Next morning. The café is full of bright sun.

Beth sits at a table looking stunned.

Behind the counter the waiter is pestering the waitress who is trying to wash dishes.

WAITER: I wanna show you something. Come on, come on, I wanna show you something. I wanna show you this trick.

WAITRESS (*raising fingers to temples*): Show it to your wife.

WAITER: No, come on, come on, I wanna show you this trick, I won't hurt you, I promise I won't hurt you.

Vicki appears at the door, still dressed as on the previous night. She does not immediately come in, but stands at the doorway in a very high state, trembling, trying to control herself.

Beth sees her, and registers her presence without change of expression. Her face is stiff.

Vicki approaches and stands beside the table.

BETH (*blankly*): Didn't you come home last night.

VICKI (*in a breathless rush*): I just want you to know that I've dug my grave and now I'm going to lie in it.

BETH (*with a hard laugh, turning her head slowly to the window and back again*): Oh, come off it.

VICKI (*still standing*): We didn't think you'd take it like this. JP said, 'She's been around. She can cope with things.'

BETH (*very level*): You've broken my heart, Vicki.

VICKI (*flustered*): JP says I'll break *his* if I change my mind.

Vicki is standing like a schoolgirl being carpeted by the headmistress: hands clasped behind her, feet together.

BETH: How could you do it? (*Her self-control is ghastly.*)

Vicki draws herself up as if about to respond to an expected challenge: this is the rationalisation she has prepared and learnt by heart.

VICKI: The question is: am I always going to stand back and not take what I want, just because it's yours?

BETH (*at first controlled*): The worst thing, you know, is when you look back. When what you thought was solid ground behind you—just—just—*crumbles.*

Beth's facade cracks. She struggles to her feet but Vicki pushes past the chair and dashes forward with her arms out.

VICKI: Oh, I want to kiss you.

She seizes Beth, puts her face in Beth's neck. Even now she takes the posture of one who wants to be comforted. They

115

are both crying. Beth embraces her, but then lets go and steps away.

BETH: That's enough. Don't come near me again. I can't help you. I can't do anything to help you any more.

She picks up her bag and walks out of the café.

———————————

JP is in the bedroom by himself, in a chaos of half-sorted belongings, with a suitcase open on the bed. He stands there with a cassette in each hand. He puts both of them into the case, then pauses, then takes one out and puts it back on the shelf.

———————————

Saturday morning.

Tim and Annie are playing the piano. Beth approaches, and stands behind them.

BETH: You two might have noticed there's a bit of drama going on round here.

ANNIE (*looks up brightly*): No! Is there?

BETH: It's about JP and Vicki. They're in love, it seems. And they want to be together.

116

Annie bursts into childish tears of shock.

Tim sits still, then walks out of the room.

ANNIE (*stopping crying suddenly as children do*): Is Vicki home?

BETH: They've gone out looking for a house.

ANNIE (*in surprised, confused tone*): I don't feel much, yet. I feel like being practical.

She looks down at the keyboard; she's in shock.

ANNIE: I should be able to play this piece by now. I ought to practise more. I ought to become a more reliable person.

Beth says nothing.

ANNIE: Do we have to move? Where will everybody live?

BETH: We'll stay here.

ANNIE (*confused*): Who will?

BETH: You and me. And Tim.

ANNIE: Maybe he won't want to.

BETH: We'll need him. For the rent.

ANNIE: Maybe he'd rather live with an ordinary family.

BETH: You can ask him, sweetheart.

ANNIE (*functioning on automatic*): Let's go to the market. Let's get some new cups. You've smashed all the blue ones.

BETH (*wildly*): Let's buy a whole new set.

ANNIE: *I* know! Let's get a *puppy*!

They start to laugh, half-hysterical, on the edge of tears.

ANNIE (*calming down*): When are they leaving?

BETH: As soon as they find a place.

ANNIE (*sternly*): I think it's silly. It won't work.

Beth shrugs.

ANNIE: Shouldn't you fight back or something? Isn't that what women are supposed to do?

Beth looks at her for a moment before speaking.

BETH: Do you know what? It's almost a relief.

Several days later, JP and Beth are walking beside the water. JP picks up a stone and throws it at the cliff, aiming at a hole in the rock. Beth picks up another and copies him. They fall into competition, jostling each other like children playing. Their faces are shadowy.

JP: If anyone looks down from one of those houses they would not guess we are a couple splitting up. They would say, 'Look at these two lovers'. (*He shouts defiantly.*) LE COUPLE SÉPARÉ DE L'ANNÉE!!! (*SEPARATED COUPLE OF THE YEAR!*)

He throws another stone.

BETH: I loved Vicki. I used to love her so much it hurt me to look at her.

JP: Yes—but you didn't love *me*.

BETH: I did! I did love you!

JP: But you didn't *notice* me. I have been for years *lonely*. I thought you were ashamed of me.

BETH: Ashamed?

JP (*in a tone much gentler than the words*): You were proud. I have made you humble.

BETH (*wildly—she is seeing what she's lost*): Our marriage was bad. It was really bad. It was hardly even a marriage at all. How could you call *that* a marriage?

JP (*half laughing*): Well, if we are not married, how can we be separating?

Beth can't help laughing at his 'logic'.
Pause. They chuck stones.

BETH: If you have a baby with her, it'll be related to me. I'll be its auntie.

She throws a stone.

BETH: It's probably against the *law*. *Some* kind of law, anyway.

JP: I don't expect...perhaps she will not stay with me for long. She is looking for experience.

He drops his stone and walks away. Beth runs to catch up with him.

JP: It's not that I *want* to leave.

BETH: But you have to. Because now everything is smashed.

She takes his hand.

BETH (*starting to cry*): Your hands are always warm. What am I going to do without your warm hands?

The back door is open and Beth is sweeping the yard with a straw broom, working hard.

Wind is blowing through the open gate.

Past her staggers JP with the last carton of stuff in his arms: on top of it, the saucepan in which the last meal (after the naturalisation ceremony) was served.

He disappears out the gate.

Annie is sitting on the stairs, halfway up, watching.

JP comes back empty-handed, and stops in front of Beth at the foot of the stairs. Annie comes down the stairs and stands right behind Beth, as if in support.

Beth and JP look at each other without speaking. Beth steps back to allow JP and Annie to say goodbye. Annie and JP put their arms round each other. Then Annie, trying not to cry, runs off into the house.

JP and Beth kiss formally, in the French way: a kiss on each cheek. They hug, then step apart.

The same morning, Vicki stands holding a broom in the kitchen of a newly rented house. Unpacked boxes are all around her. The stains of previous occupants' lives will have to be cleaned off these walls.

JP, carrying his carton, enters and watches her, unobserved.

Her face is clouded. So is his.

———————————

Tim and Annie are at the piano, working away at 'Donna Lee': stumbling, concentrating, working at the same passage over and over.

ANNIE (*ready to give up*): Oh, it's hopeless—I always make the same mistake!

TIM: No, no—it's good. It's getting better. Now we'll go back to the beginning and start again.

His hands are poised: he counts them in:
 · Two, three, four—

———————————

Beth is sitting by herself at the top of the steps. The wind is blowing through the swept, empty yard. Music from the living room can be heard faintly from here.

The telephone rings. She does not answer it.

She gets up, goes down the stairs and heads out the back gate, walking in a resolute way.

As she goes out, the camera rises and moves so that we can see her walking away down the lane.

She walks to the bottom of the lane, turns the corner into the street, and disappears.

The camera keeps rising, finds the cypress trees, and holds them.

THE END

TWO FRIENDS

screenplay by
HELEN GARNER

directed by
JANE CAMPION

produced by
JAN CHAPMAN

for the
Australian Broadcasting Corporation

CAST LIST

CO-LEADS

LOUISE	Emma Coles
KELLY	Kris Bidenko

PERFORMERS

JENNY	Kris McQuade
JIM	Stephen Leeder
FATHER	John Sheerin
MATTHEW	Sean Travers
ALISON	Kerry Dwyer
PHILIP	Martin Armiger
CHRIS	Debra May
MALCOLM	Peter Hehir
LITTLE HELEN	Lisa Rogers
KATE	Amanda Frederickson
CHARLIE	Tony Barry
KEVIN	Steve Bisley
UNIFORM SHOP ASSISTANT	Lorna King
RENATO	Giovanni Marangoni
WALLY	Rory Delaney
WOMAN	Elizabeth Gentle
PRINCIPAL	Lynne Murphy
SOULA	Emily Stocker
TEACHERS	Sher Guhl, Neil Campbell

SYNOPSIS

Louise and Kelly are two fourteen-year-old friends. Their story is told in five separate periods—over one year, moving backwards in time towards childhood.

NOTE

In this version of *Two Friends*, Louise's mother is called Jenny, while in the film itself her name is Janet. I have made this change here in order to avoid confusion with another Janet, a character in a later novel, *Cosmo Cosmolino* (1992). My double use of the name was completely accidental, though no doubt it has a meaning.

PART ONE

___

JULY 1985

It's ten o'clock on a winter morning.

A white station wagon with tinted windows turns into the carpark of a city motel. It parks and Jenny and Jim get out. He is wearing a dark suit and tie, she is dressed in unremarkable winter clothes: boots, skirt, a jumper. They walk into the building without speaking to each other.

___

Jenny and Jim approach the desk of the motel. Behind it are two women, one about fifty, an experienced-looking office worker, the other only a teenager; they are engaged in office tasks. Jenny and Jim glance at each other to see who will speak first.

JIM (*hesitates*): Whereabouts is the...um...wake?

GIRL: Up there. Turn right at the top.

The couple head for the stairs.

GIRL: Who's it for?

WOMAN: Some girl.

GIRL: I didn't see anything in the paper.

WOMAN: It's not news any more, that kind of thing. Poor kid.

GIRL: What is a wake, anyway?

Jenny and Jim enter a soulless convention room. A table is set with casks of wine, glasses, cups, an urn, plates of sandwiches; formal flower arrangements, a visitors' book. People are standing around, the kind of people who don't look comfortable dressed up. Greetings are quiet, emotional, but people are smiling. Several teenagers lean against a wall, smoking in a tearing, amateurish way.

A couple, obviously parents of the dead girl, are receiving people at the centre of the room. They have the odd, swollen, glowing eyes of people in an extreme emotional state barely controlled. The mother has a gold chain round one ankle, under her stocking; otherwise they are conservatively dressed.

Jenny and Jim get themselves a drink. They are awkward, standing about. People they know greet them: people who are clearly no longer their close friends.

WOMAN: Haven't seen you two together for donkey's years.

Jenny and Jim stand together, side by side, and talk without looking at each other: not through hostility, but rather through long years of familiarity, a sense of unthinking solidarity between them, although they parted long ago.

JENNY: How can people bear it?

JIM: I don't suppose they can.

JENNY: Do you ever try to imagine if Louise…

JIM (*he knows what she means and cuts across her in a light, tense voice*): Look—if Louise died, if anything happened to her, I'd try and be thankful that she'd already had a good crack at life. I'd try to think about that.

Pause. They drink and look around. This exchange has upset them. Jim is smiling but breathing slightly too fast.

JENNY: I've got to get her a new case for the French horn.

JIM: What's that worth?

JENNY: Heaps. A bomb.

JIM: Gawd. Still…

JENNY: But it is important, isn't it?

JIM (*alarmed*): You don't think she's at risk, do you?

JENNY: Course not. You know she's not.

JIM: But they're all at risk, aren't they. Maybe you can't tell till it's too late.

JENNY: Louise is *all right*.

JIM: What about her mate, though. The sexy one.

JENNY: Kelly's dropped out of sight.

JIM: Is she all right?

JENNY: I don't know. I don't think so.

Jim sees the dead girl's father momentarily free, and puts his glass down.

JIM: Come on, Jenny.

He walks up to the father, who turns. It takes a second for the penny to drop.

FATHER: Jim. Oh, mate.

Jim puts his arms round the father. Jenny stands aside watching. They all stand still. The two men separate.

JENNY: I loved what you said about her at the church.

Father nods, can't speak.

JENNY: We hadn't seen her for so long.

The father controls himself with an effort. He leans forward, takes their hands. He speaks with difficulty, urgently, in a low, harsh voice.

FATHER: Listen. Listen. Everybody's sad. Everybody's grieving. But when people who've got a daughter come up to me...I can see the terror in their eyes.

They do not answer. They nod, and step back. Someone else approaches the father. Jim and Jenny walk away. The father calls after them.

FATHER: Jimmy! I'm sorry I didn't go over the fence with you that day at the Springboks.

He is weeping. His face is screwed up.

———————————

Late that afternoon: the empty sand at Bondi Beach.

Kelly steps off the beach with a fairly horrible looking bloke, Panky. Kelly is dressed in full regalia: hair gelled, white make-up, tube skirt, huge holey jumper, torn fishnet stockings, pointed flat shoes, all in black. Something tied round her head.

Panky is Anglo-Saxon, pale, weedy, weak-looking; looks as if he might turn nasty. Kelly seems the stronger of the two. They set off up the street together. Their demeanour is that of people who've been together some time. They walk to a bus stop. A bus comes and Kelly steps towards it.

PANKY: See you about ten.

He does not wait for the bus to pull away but turns and walks off.

The same afternoon.

Jenny is leaning out of the upstairs bedroom window of her house. She sees Louise in school uniform come struggling down the street from the bus, lugging the French horn.

JENNY (*shouts*): Louise! Matthew's here to see you. He's downstairs.

Louise's face: interested but not pleased. She disappears with the horn through the back gate.

Louise enters the lounge room. Matthew is standing beside the table, as if not sure whether he's welcome. He is a rather soft-looking boy, tall and fair, with a fashionable haircut, not good looking. Louise is half-pleased, half-cross to see him. She greets him brusquely, and leaves him standing there while she goes to get something to eat, as kids do mechanically on returning from school: peels a mandarin and stuffs it in, but does not offer him one. They sit at the table. Conversation is awkward: Louise has little hostly charm.

MATTHEW: How's school?

LOUISE: Oh, pretty foul.

Pause.

MATTHEW: I've been to the Ballroom a few times lately.

LOUISE: I hate the Ballroom. People just walk around and pretend to be half dead and listen to foul bands.

MATTHEW: Guess who I saw down there.

LOUISE: Who?

MATTHEW: Kelly.

LOUISE (*pretends to be less interested than she is*): What did she look like?

Jenny comes in. Matthew stands up, revealing his upbringing. Jenny walks through the room.

JENNY: Anyone want a cup of tea?

MATTHEW: Yes, please.

LOUISE: I've got to start my homework. } simultaneously

Jenny disappears into the kitchen.

MATTHEW: She sent you her love.

LOUISE (*coldly*): Thanks.

Pause.

LOUISE: What did she look like?

MATTHEW: All right.

He shrugs; like many boys he is not good at the kind of detail Louise is after.

LOUISE: Oh, come on!

MATTHEW: *What?*

LOUISE: How did she *look?*

MATTHEW: How do you mean?

LOUISE: What was she wearing, for example?

MATTHEW: I didn't really notice.

Pause.

LOUISE: Did she tell you her address?

MATTHEW: Oh, she's not *living* anywhere.

Pause.

LOUISE: But where does she sleep?

MATTHEW: They're squatting. In an old fruitshop. She said it was really nice inside.

LOUISE: Who's 'they'?

MATTHEW: She was with a bloke.

LOUISE: What sort of a bloke?

MATTHEW: I think his name was Panky.

LOUISE: Yes, but what *sort* of bloke?

Matthew makes a big effort to remember some details.

MATTHEW: Quite old. About twenty. He was wearing a singlet. They were on acid. They *said* they were.

We get the impression that a lot of Matthew's knowledge of the ways of the world is pure bluff.

Jenny enters as he mentions the acid; she's carrying milk and cups.

JENNY (*lightly*): Do you mean to say people still do acid?

MATTHEW (*clearly bluffing now—repeating things he's heard*): I think they mix it with other things. Bourbon, or serepax or something.

JENNY: Who are you talking about?

MATTHEW: Kelly.

JENNY: *Kelly.* (*She steps closer.*) Is Kelly all right?

MATTHEW (*wary of another interrogation*): I think so.

JENNY (*interrogating*): Is she—you know—thin? What did her skin look like? Did you look at her eyes?

LOUISE: Oh *Mum.* Don't *embarrass* me.

MATTHEW: I didn't notice. Sorry. I think she had a bruise on her face. Just here. (*Points to his jaw.*) Can I put a record on?

Jenny goes out to the kitchen.

Matthew goes to the stereo and starts to sort through the records. Pulls one out.

MATTHEW: Nic *Kershaw.*

LOUISE (*hastily*): That's not mine. It's Mum's.

Later the same afternoon, Louise sits in school uniform at the dining room table doing her maths homework. She is alone in the orderly room. The window looks out over the street. There are underclothes drying on the heater. Other kids pass, evidently students at the local high school—not in uniform, but dressed in bright exaggerated clothes. Their voices can be heard through the closed window; staccato speech full of fuck this and fuck that; laughter in bursts.

Louise plugs on with her work. She does not even look up. A boy jumps up, in passing, to look in: his head pops up comically over the window sill.

An open box of Kleenex sits on the table beside the neat ruler and pencilcase.

Meanwhile, in the city, Kelly gets off a bus. She walks past the town hall. She posts a letter. She walks purposefully towards another bus stop: she clearly has a destination.

———————————

Early the same evening, Louise is sorting things in her bedroom. She has her head in the cupboard. Jenny stands at the door with an apron on.

LOUISE: She's a bitch. She never rings up. She said she was coming to the concert on my birthday and she never turned up. I bought her a ticket and everything. I *paid* for that ticket.

JENNY: Maybe she had a reason.

LOUISE: *And* she took my flower press and never brought it back.

JENNY: Surely neither of you is likely to be needing a flower press.

LOUISE: That's not the point. Nanna gave it to me. It's mine. Stupid moll.

JENNY: Louise! What a way to talk!

LOUISE (*reckless; almost in tears*): I don't care. She's hardly a person any more.

Kelly goes into a big chemist shop and examines some vases. They are ugly and cheap. She considers them carefully, counts her money, chooses one and takes it to the counter.

CHEMIST (*in a friendly tone, despite her outlandish appearance*): For yourself, is it?

KELLY (*hostile*): No—why?

CHEMIST (*pauses to control irritation*): If it's a present I can wrap it for you.

KELLY (*mollified*): Oh. Thanks. It's for my mother. It's her birthday.

He wraps it. She fiddles with things on a nearby shelf. He keeps an eye on her.

She takes the parcel and goes out of the shop.

That evening, Jenny and her friend Alison are standing in Jenny's kitchen. Jenny is cooking. She looks upset, as if she's been talking about something and has stopped for a moment.

Alison crouches at the open fridge and fills up two unmatching glasses from a cask of wine.

JENNY (*bursts out*): *Somebody* has to pick up the load. Kids have to be looked after. Look at Kelly. What's her mother *thinking* of? How can she have just let her go? They *let* her *go*. She'll end up like that poor kid they buried this morning—dropped in the gutter. Just left there all night.

Alison listens.

JENNY: I feel responsible for Kelly.

ALISON: Oh Jenny. Don't be silly.

JENNY: I do. I should have done something.

ALISON (*flatly*): What? What could you have done?

JENNY: I don't know. Something. Gone and talked to her parents. It probably wouldn't have helped. But at least I could have tried.

ALISON: Tried what? You can't stop them, when they want to leave.

JENNY: But Kelly's such a clever girl.

ALISON: Not clever enough, evidently.

JENNY: I even thought of taking her on myself at one stage.

ALISON (*laughs*): That's ridiculous. She would have driven you bananas.

JENNY: That's what Philip said. That's what everyone said. But somebody ought to have done something. Don't you think so? What do *you* think?

Pause.

ALISON: I used to think of handing Wally over to you. To anybody.

She laughs. Jenny tries to.

ALISON (*sentimentally*): Remember them when they were little? They were like little fairy creatures—sort of sexless. Remember when Wally used to ring up Louise and play his violin to her over the phone?

Jenny goes on preparing the meal, without answering, but listening.

ALISON (*draining her glass, picking up her bag*): He busks every Saturday morning at the market. He makes a fortune. He's so *cynical*.

JENNY (*not paying attention*): Is that somebody knocking?

ALISON (*teasing*): Haven't you given him the key yet?

Alison opens the back door. Philip stands there grinning. They greet each other and she goes out the gate. Philip enters. Jenny is very pleased indeed to see him. Her greeting is slightly more enthusiastic than his.

———————

It's almost dark. Kelly in her black regalia is walking down a street, with the restricted gait of a girl wearing a hobble skirt.

She approaches a house. She opens the front door with a key and goes in.

———————

Inside the house, we see a domestic scene: almost a tableau. In spite of the fact that it is still being renovated (which seems a permanent state, in this house: a ladder, bags of cement against a wall, a long piece of heavy timber leaning in the corner), on this evening it is warm and comfortable: curtains are drawn, a heater is going, TV on the news but the sound turned down low.

At the table sit Malcolm, Kate, Chris and little Helen. They are laughing. On top of the fridge we can see a round chocolate cake with unlit candles stuck in it. Chris is standing up with a ladle ready to dish out soup. Her back is to the door that leads into the hall. This door opens, soundlessly. Kelly appears. At first no one sees her. Then little Helen spots her and jumps up with a cry of pleasure.

LITTLE HELEN: Kelly!

We see Chris's face: a flash of delight, then she turns and sees the apparition in torn black holding a small parcel. The sight is a shock to Chris: it wounds her.

Malcolm sees Chris's reaction. He is dark-faced with fury.

MALCOLM: What the hell are you doing back here?

The room is frozen.

Chris puts down the ladle and makes as if to push back her chair and go to Kelly. But Malcolm gets to his feet in such a way as to cut off Chris's access to Kelly. Kate and little Helen are speechless.

KELLY: Mum?

She is waiting for her mother to stick up for herself, to push past the barrier of Malcolm; she is making a direct appeal.

MALCOLM (*takes a few steps towards her*): Look at yourself. You're a deadbeat.

Little Helen jumps up and darts past Malcolm: she flings her arms round Kelly's hips. Malcolm strides after her and pulls her away by one arm, as if from something that will contaminate her. Chris tries to stand up, utters the beginning of a word.

MALCOLM: Shutup Chris. It's your fault she's like this. You let me handle it.

KELLY: Mum?

MALCOLM: How dare you come here in that get-up? You look like a junkie. You look like a prostitute.

KELLY: I brought you something, Mum.

She holds out the parcel.

MALCOLM: Do you know what you're doing to your mother?

Kelly bends over and puts the parcel on the floor. At no stage does she acknowledge Malcolm or even that he's speaking to her. She is after Chris. Malcolm is a blockage between the girl and her mother. Kelly speaks only to Chris, she urgently needs Chris to answer but Chris can't.

KELLY: Mum? I'll come again, will I? I'll ring up.

No one speaks. Chris is like a prisoner. She is weak. Kelly puts out one foot and kicks the parcel across the floor to her mother. Then she turns and goes out. She closes the door behind her.

Outside it is now quite dark. Kelly walks away up the street.

Morning, several days later.

Jenny opens the front door of the house and goes out. She is dressed for work and carrying a briefcase. She looks for mail and finds a letter. It is addressed to Louise in a big flamboyant scrawl.

Jenny walks back into the house and props the letter on the piano, where the music stands, then goes out again, walking with purpose.

After school that afternoon, Louise lets herself into the house with a key. She dumps her bag, seizes food, and goes to the piano, where she sees the letter. She opens it eagerly. We see that it starts 'To my dear friend Louise'.

Kelly's voice-over goes more slowly than Louise's rate of silent reading, so that by the time Louise has read to the end, Kelly's voice is only halfway through. Louise puts the letter down on the table and sits at the piano. She starts to play: she spanks smartly through something mechanical. We hear the music under Kelly's voice.

KELLY (*voice-over*): 'To my dear friend Louise.

The first thing I should say is sorry for not contacting you sooner. For the last couple of months I've just needed a total break which I've had and feel much better for it. I've been living in Bondi, walking distance from the beach. Up until now I spent my time starving and totally broke. I had to wait about seven or eight weeks for the dole. It was pretty hard but I survived. I've just moved into a flat with some other people. The flat is really good with big rooms. The rent is $150 monthly which is not too bad especially when Dad is paying for it. So far so good, I'm not a junkie or a prostitute and life should be slightly easier now that I've got a place to call home.

I feel lots happier—for a while I seemed to be a manic depressant. I've been in love for about three months. That sounds typically like me. His name is Panky. I was living with him for about two and a half months, then things deteriorated but I'm hoping things will pick up again. At the moment I'm waiting for the postman who will hopefully bring a check from my father. As once again I don't have any money. I've been sick for about two weeks, probably from bad diet etc...I was on antibiotics etc...but I'm over that now. I lost my cat, she was with me and one day just disappeared. My new address is on the envelope, come and visit me any time. I haven't seen the family at all. I've been sort of holding my breath. Not sure how they will react but I'm going over there tonight which is Mum's birthday. Maybe I will get a cooked meal for once! Give my love to Soula, Julie, Justine, Jenny and that dag Matthew.

147

Take care and please write back. I'll save the rest for when I see you.

> With love,
> Kelly xxx
> PS Sorry I didn't make it to your birthday. Something came up.
> PPS Recognise the paper?'

We see Louise's face as she plays. She is almost crying.

FADE TO BLACK

———————————————

PART TWO

FIVE MONTHS EARLIER
FEBRUARY 1985

Morning, at a bus stop. Among a crowd of schoolkids, we see Louise in a very new uniform and hard black lace-up shoes, with a heavy bag on her shoulder. The bus comes. Louise and the others get on. She has to stand. She sees another pair of shiny black shoes: raises her eyes and sees another girl in the same uniform, about to start at the same new school. They smile, embarrassed, and quickly look away without speaking.

Also on the bus is Matthew, in some kind of uniform involving a blazer. Louise keeps glancing at him; he is reading something. He looks up and registers her attention—they notice each other.

An afternoon, some weeks later.
Louise and Matthew walk down the street together

from the bus. They walk with a lot of space between them. They look shy, with awkward smiles.

As they approach Louise's gate, the white station wagon with tinted windows, not in good repair, pulls up in front of the house. Jim gets out of it, and waits for them.

LOUISE: That's my Dad. Foul car, isn't it.

Matthew gives a tactful shrug. They reach the car. It has a baby seat in the back.

LOUISE: Matthew, this is my father.

Jim gives Matthew a friendly nod and a curious glance. Matthew puts out his hand and they shake.

JIM: Looks like we're visiting the same girl.

LOUISE (*mortified*): *Da*-ad.

Matthew gives an airy little wave and attempts an epigram.

MATTHEW: Great minds think alike.

He heaves his bag and wanders off. Louise looks at Jim with a soft look.

Jim and Louise are now in the lounge room. Jim is leaning on the window sill watching the schoolkids pass, while Louise unpacks her French horn and gets ready to play. Louise is chattering without expecting an answer.

LOUISE: Malcolm's so stingy, he won't even pay for her to have singing lessons. He says she has to work at the chemist after school if she wants something special. Special! I think that's *disgusting*. I think he's a bastard. He's foul.

JIM: Doesn't her mother ever stick up for her?

LOUISE: *She's* scared of him too. She's *pathetic*. He's not even her real father. I don't see why he should have the right to ruin everything.

Now she is set up and begins to tune the instrument. Jim turns in from the window.

The front door bangs and Jenny comes bustling down the hall. Friendly looks and greetings.

JENNY: Oh, hi Jimmy! Did Philip ring, Louise?

LOUISE (*casually*): No. He didn't.

Jenny forges through into the kitchen. Louise raises the French horn to her lips.

JIM (*in a conspiratorial whisper, grinning*): Who's Philip?

Louise merely raises her eyebrows. She begins to play.

That evening, Jim and Louise are at a table in a cheap and noisy restaurant, having dinner. Jim pours her half a glass and himself a full one. Obviously she thinks the sun shines out of him: she listens with rapt attention while he tells a great tale, with actions and gestures.

JIM: Of course, he's in parliament now, but I used to know him at uni. He was so horrible that he had to grow a beard to try and hide how horrible he was.

They eat. Louise, chewing, looks happily round the restaurant.

LOUISE: Hey, Dad. Do you think anyone could mistake us for girlfriend and boyfriend?

Later that night Louise is sitting up in her bed writing in her diary.

JENNY (*voice-over*): Turn that light off now.

LOUISE: In a minute.

She finishes and hides the diary behind the mirror on her dressing table.

An afternoon, some days later.

Louise and Matthew get off the bus.

Kelly (who looks a lot less extreme in dress and hair than in the first section) is leaning against a shop window with folded arms, waiting. The two girls spot each other, and dash forward; there is a lot of shrieking, hugging and kissing; they babble:—'Haven't seen you for *ages*'—'Look at those *socks*!'—'Who've you got for English?'—'Is Kennedy still there?'—'Do they go on camps?' Matthew stands apart, looks into the distance as if patiently waiting for an overdone performance to end.

Kelly is already examining Matthew with a practised eye.

LOUISE: Matthew, this is my best friend, Kelly.

Matthew and Kelly greet each other.

LOUISE: Kelly got into City Girls' too. She *should* be there if it wasn't for her bloody dickhead stepfather.

KELLY (*shrugs*): Oh, it's not too bad at King Street. Anyway... I might be leaving school after my birthday.

LOUISE (*shocked*): Leaving school?

KELLY (*bluffing*): My Dad reckons he might be able to line me up a job where he works.

Louise is absolutely stumped by this.

The same afternoon, Louise, Kelly and Matthew burst into the kitchen at Louise's place.

Kelly goes straight to the TV and turns it on, then walks away without a glance at it. Their schoolbags are dumped askew in doorways. They forage in the kitchen. Kelly is completely at home in Louise's kitchen, while Matthew politely stands back and waits to be offered food.

Their conversation is sporadic, mostly about school. Louise plays down the thrill of City Girls' so as not to make Kelly feel bad about not being there too. 'You should see the science teacher', etc.

Kelly tells about their common acquaintances. 'Justine's had a *bob*. The back of her neck's all shaved.'

They drift through a door into the lounge room. Kelly picks up a photo album with a shriek and opens it with a flourish. They all bend over it. The girls chatter about the pictures.

In this scene, Matthew is not much more than an audience for a performance by the girls of their friendship: they show him, as it were, their relics.

Matthew, not your ordinary slob, is quite entertained: he's the kind of boy who enjoys girls' company and is accepted by them.

Louise seems, in her ugly uniform, almost childlike, compared with Kelly who's dressed in coloured, sloppy, attractive clothes.

Kelly plays up to Matthew—almost as if she can't help it. (Kelly will become one of those women who, when there's a man in the room, unconsciously channel all their attention towards him.)

Kelly's small betrayal of Louise: in the photo album there is a picture of their two pink plastic orthodontic plates—a comical photo, perhaps they are on the table beside a vase of flowers or even on the edge of a swimming pool.

LOUISE: Argh! Our plates.

Louise tries to turn the page. Kelly stops her.

KELLY: Look—you can tell you've got yours in, there—you're smiling with your lips closed.

LOUISE: I look *ghastly*.

KELLY: Louise still has to put hers in, don't you Louise. Every night.

Kelly turns the page without looking at Louise, who registers the casual treachery in a tiny way. No one is looking at anyone.

Later the same afternoon, Matthew has gone home and the girls are upstairs in Louise's bedroom. Kelly is restless, roaming about looking at things, while Louise is hastily getting out of her uniform.

KELLY: I thought you said Matthew was a spunk.

Louise is thrown by this.

LOUISE (*uncertainly*): Well? He is.

KELLY: I reckon he's probably a bit of a poof.

LOUISE: He is not!

KELLY: You can always tell.

LOUISE: Why'd you say that to him, about my plate?

KELLY: Well, it's true!

LOUISE: You didn't have to say it in public.

KELLY: Who cares? He's probably got one himself. A great big pink one. With one false tooth, right in the front.

Kelly is trying to charm her. Louise can't help laughing. The mood lightens.

KELLY: Where's Jenny?

LOUISE: At work.

KELLY: Let's have a little glass of vodka before she gets back.

Louise hangs her dress and blazer behind the door.

LOUISE: You can. I have to do my homework.

KELLY: Oh, how boring.

LOUISE: I wish you'd been allowed to come to City Girls'.

KELLY: Why?

LOUISE: I just think it would've been better.

Louise sounds a bit prudish.

———————————

After dinner that evening, Jenny is driving her car across the Harbour Bridge. Louise is beside her. The radio is on the ABC: the Law Report, a sober voice talking. They don't speak to each other but seem at ease, listening and looking out the windows.

JENNY: Marvellous clouds, aren't they.

157

LOUISE: Shh. I'm listening.

At the music teacher's house, Jenny sits alone at a dining room table reading the *Sun*. The room has a modern table and chairs, a floral carpet, a sideboard with sporting cups and shields lined up; on the walls are framed photos of race horses.

From the next room we hear two horns playing in harmony: one strongly and well, the other more hesitant, following.

Jenny turns a page, reads: seems to pay no attention to the music.

———————

The same evening, in the kitchen/living room, at Kelly's house—the usual partly renovated state of flux. Though the used parts of the room are clean and orderly, it's as if chaos is always just being kept at bay. The sound of a shower pounding in the bathroom.

Kelly is slouched in front of the TV. Her mother, Chris, is cooking. Little Helen is cutting things out of paper on the floor with intense concentration.

CHRIS (*discreetly, in low voice*): The school rang up today.
They said you'd missed two days already this week.

Kelly does not answer.

CHRIS: Where do you go?

From her tone we see that she is afraid of Kelly, nervous of her. Kelly does not speak or look up.
      The shower stops. Malcolm shouts from the bathroom.

MALCOLM (*voice-over*): Chris? Chris! There are no towels here.

CHRIS: Take him a towel, Kell, will you.

KELLY: You take him one. You're his slave, not me.

CHRIS (*appealing*): Oh, Kelly.

KELLY: *He* wouldn't take *you* one! Why do you wait on him?

Malcolm's head round bathroom door.

MALCOLM: Come on! What's going on out there? I asked
      for a towel.

KELLY (*shouts*): Get your own towel like everybody else does.

Chris downs the spatula and runs out the back door for a towel off the line.

MALCOLM (*round the door*): I've had a gutful of you, Kelly.

KELLY (*still without looking at him*): Don't worry. I won't be
      here much longer. I'm going to live with Dad.

159

Chris runs in with a towel and hands it to Malcolm round the door. He takes it without looking at her and withdraws into the bathroom.

MALCOLM (*voice-over*): Don't be stupid. He doesn't want you loafing round his flat.

KELLY (*shouts*): He does so. And he's going to pay for me to have singing lessons.

Malcolm gives a loud, contemptuous laugh from the bathroom. Kelly gets up and leaves the room.

Little Helen goes on cutting and pasting throughout all this.

That night, in Kelly's bedroom which she shares with her older half-sister Kate. Kelly is lying in her bed, propped up on one elbow, reading by the bedlamp on the head of her bed. It is a book, not a comic or magazine: a fat tome, *Gone with the Wind*. Kate stirs in her sleep and turns over.

KATE: Turn the light off, will you? I've got an exam at nine o'clock in the morning.

KELLY: I'm reading.

KATE: Turn it *off*.

Kelly does so, and puts the book down on the floor. They talk in the dark.

KATE: I saw you today, Kelly.

KELLY: So what?

KATE: You want to watch out.

KELLY: Mr Kennedy already rang.

KATE: I didn't mean that.

KELLY: What *did* you mean.

KATE: You know.

KELLY: Oh, shutup.

KATE: You're stupid, Kelly.

Kelly gets out of her bed and leaves the room.

An hour later. The house is still. Kelly, in a nightie and a blanket, is sunk in a chair in front of the TV. *Gone with the Wind* lies face down beside her. Something silly is jumping on the screen.

Little Helen in pyjamas appears in the doorway. Kelly does not look up. Little Helen walks over to her, stands beside her chair and looks at the screen. She tugs Kelly by the sleeve.

LITTLE HELEN: What can this chirpy little thing do?

KELLY: Haven't you been to sleep yet?

LITTLE HELEN: I was thinking.

KELLY: What about?

LITTLE HELEN: I was thinking about cut-outs and plasticine.

KELLY: You'll be tired in the morning.

Pause.
    Little Helen gets on Kelly's lap and settles there.

LITTLE HELEN: Hey, Kelly. Do you like making things?

KELLY (*dully*): No. Not much. I used to.

LITTLE HELEN: I *love* making things. And sometimes I stay awake all night thinking about the things I'm going to make.

KELLY: You probably don't stay awake the *whole* night.

LITTLE HELEN: Yes I do.

KELLY: Till breakfast time?

LITTLE HELEN: Yep.

KELLY: I bet you drop off round three a.m.

LITTLE HELEN: No. I bet you I don't.

Their attention returns to the screen. Kelly is dull with unhappiness. Helen sits contentedly on her lap. She puts one palm against Kelly's cheek. Her eyes are glazed.

———————————

Next afternoon.

Louise and Jenny are walking along in the supermarket, trundling the trolley. Louise is telling a story, with gusto, and mimicry.

LOUISE: And then the bedroom door bursts open and out comes Malcolm in his underpants, chuckin' a mental yelling 'What is it? A DOG? A DOG?'

Jenny laughs. They enter the delicatessen.

JENNY (*with list*): And now I need two rabbits and some mustard for the sauce.

LOUISE: *Rabbits?* I hate rabbit. I refuse to eat it.

JENNY: It's exactly like chicken. Anyway you're not invited. It's adults only.

LOUISE: Thanks a lot! What am I supposed to do? Thrown out of my own house, where I live! Just so you can entertain your daggy boyfriend.

JENNY (*refusing to bite*): Go and see *your* boyfriend. Go and watch TV at *their* place.

LOUISE: Matthew is *not* my boyfriend.

JENNY: Oh go on, Louise. Be a sport. Go over to Kelly's.

LOUISE: Can't. Don't want to.

JENNY: Aren't you two friends any more?

LOUISE: Yeah, but…it's not the same.

Jenny is concentrating on the rabbits under the glass and is not really paying attention. Louise has her back turned so as not to see the little corpses.

LOUISE: Anyway. I hate dinner parties. You drink too much wine and your nose goes red and you rave on.

Jenny looks up, stung. Louise is half-smiling; she is trying

164

Jenny out, just a little flick of power to see if it works. It does, but Jenny tries to look unaffected.

LOUISE: And the way you go on about Philip. It's worse than a True Romance comic.

Louise turns away again and folds her arms. Jenny looks at her, then at the blood-stained woman who is selling the rabbits. The woman has witnessed the exchange and gives Jenny a sympathetic grimace; she makes a strangling gesture with her two hands. Jenny tries to smile.

JENNY: I'll have two of the small ones, thanks.

The woman obliges. Jenny pays. Louise stands with folded arms and face turned away, waiting. Jenny puts the parcel in the trolley and walks off. Louise follows.

That evening, Jenny is having some friends to dinner: Philip, Alison and Stephen. Music plays softly. A pleasant scene: they are having a nice time, quietly.

Jenny takes the lid off the pan that contains the main course.

JENNY: Anybody here take a moral position on rabbit?

STEPHEN: Not me. I love it.

The phone rings out in the hallway. Jenny looks up.

JENNY: Damn.

She hands the serving spoon to Philip.

JENNY: Won't be a minute.

She goes to answer, leaving the door ajar behind her. The others go on with the meal.

JENNY: Hullo? Oh, hullo, Kelly. No, she's not here at the moment. Can I take a message? She went over to Matthew's for tea. Will I get her to call you when she gets home?

She is silent, listening. From her face we see that Kelly is launching into a monologue. Jenny glances back into the living room. The others are talking and eating merrily without her. She abandons hope of a quick escape, and sits down.

JENNY: Where are you ringing from?

We see Kelly in the living room of her father, Charlie's flat. It has grey brick walls: the kind of flat that a man might rent who only comes home to sleep; but he's equipped it with what he thinks is needed, with no sense of the place being the product of gradual, organic growth—rather as if somewhere there existed a list of objects that add up to a house, and he's followed it to the letter. Good quality, new, modern-looking furniture. A bareness between things. The kitchen utensils probably still have supermarket price stickers on them. Rather desolate: not a home.

Kelly is on the phone. A door behind her gives onto a balcony which is stuffed with cardboard cartons. We can see two men out there—or parts of them, trousered legs, a back in an expensive shirt—and hear voices and laughter.

KELLY: I'm at my Dad's. No—he's here. He's out on the balcony with the other guy who's staying here. Can you hear them?

Kelly holds out the receiver towards the open door, then puts it back to her ear.

KELLY: They're having a drink. Hear that tooting? Every-time a car goes past they wave and whistle, and see if they can make them toot. (*She giggles.*)
    I might be coming to live here, actually...
    No, not all that much. He eats out a lot. Yesterday he went to the supermarket, and do you know what he came home with? A jar of vegemite and some toilet paper. I know!...Hopeless. They're so stubborn...

She laughs, woman to woman, indulging the foolishness and impracticality of men.

KELLY: Guess what—I've started singing lessons...

She's a bit of a dag...

Oh, you know—dried flowers in the hair, that style of thing...I'm supposed to do scales every day. It's all right, I s'pose...

Jenny hangs onto the phone, while the dinner continues without her.

JENNY: Listen, Kelly—I've got some people here, I'll have to go. Do you want to come over? You could wait here for Louise.

At her end, Kelly considers Jenny's offer.

Charlie sticks his head round the balcony door and waves to her. She smiles and waves back, while still talking.

KELLY: No thanks, Jenny—I'll be okay here. I've got a video to watch. *Hostesses on Heat*. No—I was only fooling. Give my love to Louise. I think she's got the shits with me a bit at the moment.

CHARLIE: Get off the phone, will you, Kell? I'm expecting a call.

Jenny, winding up now, stands as she speaks into the receiver.

JENNY: Well, if you ever need a place to stay, Kelly...Don't you sit up too late, will you. Goodnight, love.

She hangs up and goes back towards the dinner table.

ALISON: Who was it?

JENNY: Kelly.

ALISON: Is Kelly all right?

Jenny shrugs as if to say 'I don't know'. She looks at Philip. The two men are eating with gusto.

STEPHEN: Great tucker, Jenny.

Jenny picks up the bottle of wine and refills the glasses.

———————————

At Charlie's flat, the balcony door is now closed. Kelly, Charlie and Kevin are watching a video. Kelly has a glass too: they are drinking wine.
    The phone rings.
    Charlie, who is nearest, answers it.

CHARLIE (*very softly*): Hullo? Oh—hi!

From his tone and expression we see that it is a woman he is interested in.

CHARLIE: Where are you? Look, I'd love to—I really would— but my daughter's here. She's staying the night.

He is being persuaded; he puts up feeble resistance.

CHARLIE: No. Kev's here...What about tomorrow night? Won't that do?

He laughs: she is flirting with him.

CHARLIE: Okay. All right. I'm on my way. Give me twenty minutes.

Kelly glances up at this: she is surprised and hurt, but quickly hides her reaction. He does not notice.

CHARLIE: Listen, Kelly—I've got to pop out for a while—you don't mind, do you? Kev'll be here, won't you, Kev?

Kev nods.

KELLY (*blankly*): All right then.

Charlie has expected resistance; her passive acceptance throws him somewhat. He hesitates, then disappears into the bathroom; we hear the shaver.

Kelly and Kevin are careful not to look at each other. Charlie reappears in a clean shirt.

KELLY (*with peculiar blank politeness, almost like a lesson learnt*): That's a nice shirt.

Charlie glances helplessly down at himself. He bends over and kisses her on the cheek.

CHARLIE: See you in the morning, sweetheart.

KELLY (*eyes on the screen, blankly*): Okay. Goodnight.

CHARLIE: See you, Kev.

KEVIN: Righto, mate. 'Night.

Charlie goes out the door. The video finishes. There is a blank screen, and a blank moment between Kelly and Kevin. Kevin has witnessed her slight at the hands of her father. She has been humiliated by Charlie's lack of care for her. Kevin would like to be kind to her but does not quite know how. She is lonely and neglected; she is also at that unsettling stage between childhood and adult sexuality.

KEVIN: How about a game of poker.

KELLY: I don't know the rules. I'm not much good at cards.

KEVIN: I could teach you.

Kelly has a sudden idea. She sits up.

KELLY: I know. We could play Poleconomy.

KEVIN: Poleconomy? What's that?

Kelly bounces to her school bag and gets out a large flat box. She sets up the boardgame on the table. Kevin is dismayed but hides it out of politeness: he thinks he is in for some childish boredom. Kelly sets up the board. Her mood has changed. She begins to explain the rules to him. Seeing the rules are those of business practice, he knows them already from practical experience. He decides to relax into it, and sits back with a smile to witness her performance. She goes on and on, her voice becomes more confident as she goes. Kevin takes up his money and gets ready to play. There is something touching about her long and detailed explanation: he is getting interested in her. She notices this, and begins quite subtly to play up to him.

She is sexually vulnerable, but she is not completely innocent. It comforts her ego, it excites and flatters her to be the object of his attention. Kevin's expression is at the same time tender, amused and knowing. They communicate in looks and angles of body language and smiles and pauses.

After midnight, the same night. The living room of Charlie's flat is in darkness. Kelly is asleep on the couch.

She wakes up. Someone has put a blanket over her. She is fully dressed. She gets up and walks along the hall to the lavatory.

———————

Meanwhile, in Kevin's bedroom, he is only half-asleep. He sits up. We hear the toilet being flushed. Light goes off. We hear Kelly feeling her way back down the passage.

KEVIN: That you, Charlie?

Kelly appears in doorway.

KELLY: No. It's me.

KEVIN: Is he back yet?

KELLY: No.

Silence. She stands there.

KEVIN: Are you all right?

KELLY: Yes. I'm all right.

Pause.

KEVIN: Do you want to come in here for a minute?

Pause.

Kelly sighs.

KEVIN: What's wrong?

KELLY: Nothing.

KEVIN: Come in here.

Kelly walks slowly in and sits on the edge of the bed.

Silence.

Kevin moves over and lifts up the bedclothes. He's got on a T-shirt and underpants. She gets in. He puts his arms around her. She submits. He behaves quite gently towards her: as a comforter. Then he kisses her on the mouth.

Kevin may be an opportunist but he is not a *rapist*. However, his behaviour towards her is deeply ambiguous. He is *in loco parentis*. He is breaking a taboo.

Kelly goes along with it for a few minutes. She seems to be enjoying it, but then things get a bit hot for her. She feels him change gear and start to mean business.

In a sudden burst of panic or revulsion Kelly pushes him away. She struggles out into the lounge and turns on the overhead light. The blaze of harsh light dispels all subtlety or romance. Kelly is white, almost gagging. She pulls on her shoes, heads for the front door, opens it, comes back, looks round wildly, spots her schoolbag, heaves it onto her shoulder and bolts. Kevin appears in the hallway.

KEVIN: Don't go, Kelly! I'm sorry!

Twenty minutes later.

Kelly is walking fast along a city footpath, her school-bag over her shoulder. There is hardly any traffic. There is no one in the street. She looks behind her, and breaks into a run.

A soft, insistent knocking.

Jenny stumbles to her front door in the dark, pulling on a dressing gown. She opens the door uncertainly. Kelly is crouching on the doorstep with her bag, panting.

JENNY: Is that you, Kelly?

KELLY (*standing up*): There weren't any cars. I thought someone was after me. I ran and ran—a man came round the corner and he—

JENNY (*confused*): He *what*?

KELLY: He was—

There is a shuffling in the hall behind Jenny. Kelly stops short. They turn and see Louise, stunned with sleep, standing halfway down the stairs in her nightie. Kelly takes a big breath and pulls herself together, she and Jenny exchange a look: this conversation can't continue in front of Louise who is more innocent than both of them.

Jenny and Kelly at this moment have a perfect, wordless understanding.

LOUISE (*blurred*): Hi, Kelly! Where are you going?

KELLY: Nowhere.

Kelly puts her bag down.

LOUISE: Can she stay the night, Mum?

JENNY: Of course she can. It's one o'clock in the morning, for God's sake. Go up and get in my bed. I'll make us a cup of tea.

LOUISE: Come on.

Louise turns and goes back up the stairs. Kelly picks up her bag and follows. Jenny heads for the kitchen.

The girls enter Jenny's bedroom, which is orderly and rather bare. Louise plunges straight back into bed.

Kelly stands looking at the bed. On the bedside table is Louise's dental plate.

KELLY: Do you still *sleep* with her?

176

LOUISE (*abashed*): I was reading in here and I dropped off.

Kelly dumps her bag and starts to get undressed.

LOUISE: Where have you been?

KELLY: Just out.

Kelly leaves her T-shirt and underpants on and gets in.

KELLY: Where's Jenny going to sleep?

LOUISE: She can have my bed.

Kelly lies down. A moment's silence.

KELLY: Put your plate in. Your teeth will never be straight.

Louise reaches out and gets the plate, puts it in with a clack. She turns her back to Kelly and snuggles her bum towards her. Kelly rolls onto her side and puts one arm round Louise.

LOUISE (*already drowsy again*): Goodnight Kelly.

KELLY: Goodnight.

LOUISE: I can feel your heart beating. Have you been running or something?

KELLY: Shh. Go to sleep.

Afternoon, several days later.

    Louise in uniform leans out the window of her house. She sees Matthew and Kelly walk past. They are walking quickly, heads down, in urgent conversation. They don't see her. They don't even look up.

FADE TO BLACK

PART THREE

ONE MONTH EARLIER
JANUARY 1985

Morning.

Louise and Jenny are in the school uniform department of a city store.

Jenny has a couple of gingham dresses over her arm and a pleated skirt with the stitches still in the hem. They are looking at the blazers. Both are in a bad temper. Louise is almost tearful.

LOUISE: I don't know why they have to put those revolting stiff collars on the white shirts. They'll never soften up.

JENNY (*not looking at her*): The way *you* treat your clothes, they'll be in tatters by the end of first term. My God. Look at this. *$75* for the blazer. It's bloody daylight robbery.

The shop assistant, a woman in her fifties, approaches.

JENNY (*getting in gear*): Why are school clothes so expensive? This blazer. $75. If it was lined I could understand it. But it's *thin*. It's not even going to keep her warm.

SHOP ASSISTANT (*suavely rearranging hangers on a rack*): If it was lined, madam, it wouldn't *be* a blazer. If it had a lining, it would be a jacket.

Jenny glances at Louise for solidarity, but Louise is furious and won't be in it.

JENNY (*to assistant*): We'll try these on, thank you.

———————————

Jenny is leaning against the wall of the little passageway outside the fitting rooms. She is holding a blazer, a winter skirt, two white shirts and a gingham dress.

Meanwhile, inside the fitting room, Louise is struggling into a gingham dress. She buttons it up and stares at herself in the mirror.

JENNY (*voice-over, from outside*): Does it fit?

LOUISE: It's the right length.

Jenny pushes in through the curtain. She takes a look at the dress.

JENNY: Oh, don't be silly. You'll have to get the next size bigger. Here.

Hands her the other dress.

LOUISE: But I like *this* one.

JENNY: The waist's right up under your armpits!

Louise snatches the other dress and holds it up against her.

LOUISE: It's daggy. I'm going to look a dag in it.

JENNY: Oh, stop mucking round and try it on.

LOUISE: I'm *waiting* for you to *go outside.*

Jenny goes outside. Louise, with excruciating modesty, changes dresses. This one's waist is in the right place but the hem is halfway down her calves. She looks at herself in sullen despair.

JENNY (*voice-over, from outside*): Have you got it on?

Louise doesn't answer. Jenny sticks her head in, and enters.

JENNY (*briskly*): Oh, that's miles better. You can grow into that one.

LOUISE (*almost in tears*): It's foul. If you think I'm going out on the public street wearing *this*—

181

JENNY: Oh, for God's sake, Louise—I'll take up the hem when we get home!

Jenny charges out.

We see Louise slowly taking off the dress and putting her ordinary clothes back on. At the same time we can hear Jenny speaking to the shop assistant in the charming tone mothers use to others even after they've just been growling at their child.

SHOP ASSISTANT (*voice-over*): It's always wisest to buy the bigger size. I think you'll find she'll soon grow into it.

JENNY (*voice-over*): She's small for her age. I'm sure she's about to shoot up any minute now.

Louise examines herself in the mirror. She is ill-tempered, mutinous, miserable, helpless.

————————————

An hour later Louise and Jenny stand waiting with a pile of books at the cash register of a big secondhand bookshop.
    Jenny spots Kelly on the far side of the shop.

JENNY: Hey, look who's here!

Louise sees Kelly. Jenny goes to call to Kelly; Louise grabs her sleeve.

LOUISE: Shut*up*!

JENNY: What?

LOUISE: I don't want her to see the uniform.

But too late. Kelly has seen them and approaches.

KELLY: Hi, Jenny! Ooh, I *love* your shirt—it's *gorgeous*. What've you two been buying?

Louise decides to brazen it out, and hands her the bags. Kelly rummages; pulls out one shoe, an ugly black lace-up with square toes. She holds it up and makes a great play of examining it from every angle.

LOUISE: They're awful. They're *disgusting*.

KELLY: You poor thing. Imagine having to clomp along the street in those.

Louise takes it and hastily puts it back in the bag. Jenny meanwhile is forking out more money for the books.

———————————

Early that afternoon, Louise, Kelly and Jenny, loaded with parcels and bags, travel home in a bus. Louise and Kelly sit together in a double seat, Jenny is in the seat behind. Jenny is examining the textbooks. She leans forward to the girls.

JENNY: Hey, this is interesting—listen: (*She reads out a sentence.*)

LOUISE (*embarrassed*): Shutup, Mum! You're so *loud*!

Jenny, rebuked, sits back and goes silent.

LOUISE: Oh, what's the *matter*.

JENNY: I hate it when you speak to me like that.

LOUISE: Tsk. Oh, sor*ree*.

Louise and Kelly exchange a glance of complicity.
Jenny looks out the window. She is hurt. The girls in front of her (we see the backs of their heads) are chattering brightly—we can't hear what they're saying. Jenny is excluded.
Louise turns round and speaks to her.

LOUISE: Mum, can Kelly stay the night?

JENNY (*pretending not to be hurt*): Yes, I suppose so. I'm going out for tea. She'd better ring her mother when we get home.

KELLY: Oh, they won't mind. They've gone away for the weekend.

Early one afternoon, in Jenny's kitchen, Louise and Kelly are washing up. They begin to sing, something they've learnt at school. They are busy with their task and don't look at each other. A pretty, simple harmony, a traditional tune.

It is not a performance. It is casual. Kelly with the rubber gloves on slings some coffee grounds out the window without breaking the rhythm.

They are at ease with each other: it's a common activity, a remnant of less complicated times.

It is mid-afternoon, a hot summer day at the baths.

Louise and Kelly emerge from a changing shed.

We see that Kelly is physically much more developed than Louise, and flaunts it, while Louise is slender and bony, and keeps a towel round her shoulders in that shawl-like way of small girls.

In the best position on the steps is a group of rougher-looking teenagers.

KELLY: Hey, look—there's Renato.

Louise glances, then looks away, but Kelly waves. The girls lay out their towels and bags.

––––––––––––––––

Louise and Kelly are in the water, bobbing about. Kelly is trying to keep her hair dry. Louise doesn't care. She splashes.

KELLY: Look *out*! It'll go all flat.

LOUISE (*keenly*): Want to swim up and down?

KELLY: I might just go and say hullo to Renato and them. Back in a minute.

Kelly swims away, keeping her head up. Louise begins serious swimming.

––––––––––––––––

Louise climbs out of the pool and returns to their towels. She dries herself carefully, fluffs up her hair, stretches out on the towel. Gets a book out of her bag and begins to read. It is a school English text: *Jane Eyre*.

She glances over at the group. Kelly is mucking around with Renato and others. Hoarse cries, laughter (also our first sighting of Sam, who will appear later that evening). Louise goes back to her book.

A shadow falls on her.

WALLY: Hi, Louise.

Louise looks up. A skinny, prepubescent boy is standing there.

LOUISE: Hullo, Wally.

She is not interested, but he does not notice and sits down.

WALLY: Isn't Kelly here?

LOUISE: She's over there.

WALLY: Oh…I was wondering if you wanted to busk at the market.

LOUISE (*cool*): I don't think a French horn and a violin would go all that well together. I'd drown you out.

WALLY: We could take it in turns. I make a lot of money.

LOUISE: How much?

WALLY: I made about thirteen bucks last Saturday.

Louise is keeping a finger on the place in the book.

LOUISE: What sort of stuff do you play?

WALLY: Oh, showtunes mostly. Shit. That's what they like to hear. Corny stuff. 'Feelings'. 'Be a Clown', 'Don't Cry for Me Argentina'.

LOUISE: I don't know any of those songs.

She looks back at her book. Wally is dismissed. After a moment he gets up.

WALLY: See you, Louise.

LOUISE (*without looking up*): Bye.

_____

Later the same afternoon, Louise and Kelly are walking home from the baths.

LOUISE (*hurt and angry*): You just dumped me.

KELLY: Oh, sorree! You should've come over.

She is all jangly and hyped up from the social and sexual attention; she tries to charm Louise out of her sulk.

KELLY: I was dying for a smoke.

LOUISE (*bursts out*): You look like a dickhead when you smoke. The way you hang your head back. (*Mimics her.*) I *know* you, Kelly. You can't impress *me*.

Silence. They walk.

KELLY: I am *absolutely* starving.

———————————

Early that evening Jenny is at the stove in her kitchen. Louise and Kelly enter, looking cocky and comradely.

LOUISE: What are *you* doing here? I thought you were going out with Philip.

JENNY: He didn't feel like going out. There's some spaghetti here—want to sit up?

LOUISE: We've already eaten, thanks.

JENNY (*surprised*): What did you have?

KELLY: We went up to Marcellino's.

JENNY: But you didn't have any money.

LOUISE: I know. We conned a free meal.

JENNY: You *conned* it?

LOUISE: Kelly knows the waiter.

KELLY: We had rigatoni. One. With two forks.

Jenny is disapproving, miffed. Plays the martyr a bit.

JENNY: I've obviously been wasting my time, then.

She puts down the spoon, turns off the gas and flounces out of the room towards the stairs.

KELLY: Do you mind if I make a phone call?

JENNY: Go ahead.

Louise opens the freezer and peers in, looking for ice-cream.
	Kelly is on the phone. We hear her voice murmuring, she gives an intimate laugh.

LOUISE (*shouts*): Do you want chopped nuts on yours?

KELLY (*shouts*): Yes, please.

Kelly bounces back into the living room and sits on the sofa.

———————————

Five minutes later.
	Jenny is lying on her bed reading. She hears the front door-knocker and footsteps running to answer.

———————————

Downstairs, Louise passes through the kitchen door-way into the lounge room with a bowl in each hand: fancy ice-cream, all covered with topping, nuts, whipped cream, etc.

She stops when she sees there is now a boy in the living room, standing with Kelly as if about to sit on the couch with her.

KELLY: Sam, this is Louise.

Sam is about twenty, Italian, presentable-looking. We have already glimpsed him at the baths.

SAM: Hullo.

Sam has the blank look of someone determined not to notice the untowardness of the situation: he's narrowed his sights to what will happen between him and Kelly.

Louise stands still, holding the plates.

KELLY: Sit down. Make yourself comfortable.

Sam does so. She sits beside him.

Louise goes back off into the kitchen, puts the plates down, opens the back door and goes out.

Louise is standing in the backyard. It is dark. The kitchen door behind her is open; light spills out.

A few minutes later, Jenny enters the lounge room on her way to the kitchen. She sees the back view of two heads on the couch: Kelly and Sam with his arm around her. Jenny keeps walking.

———————————

In the backyard, Louise is still just standing there. Jenny comes out the back door.

JENNY: Who's that in there?

LOUISE: Kelly and Sam.

JENNY: Who's Sam?

LOUISE: I think he's a hairdresser.

JENNY: Where'd *he* spring from?

LOUISE: She met him at the baths. He knows Renato.

They stand helplessly in the yard. TV faintly from inside.
    They are almost giggling.

JENNY: What'll we do? I feel furious.

LOUISE: We could water the pot plants.

A pause. The dark yard. The sound of a car passing. The flyscreen rattles. Kelly comes out the back door. She speaks courteously to Jenny.

KELLY: Jenny, do you mind about Sam?

Jenny is disarmed by Kelly's directness.

JENNY: You didn't even introduce him to me.

Pause.

KELLY: Would you rather we left?

JENNY: Oh Kelly—I wish you'd asked me first.

Kelly goes up and kisses Jenny on the cheek.

KELLY: I'm sorry. We'll go.

She does not speak to Louise, but turns and goes back into the house.

———————————

Louise and Jenny enter the lounge room from the kitchen. The front door is heard to close.

The TV is still on. On the low table stand two half-empty glasses of whisky.

The same evening. Now, in the lounge room, music is playing, a serious mezzo singing.

Louise is standing on the dinner table with the new uniform dress on. Jenny is pinning it up.

Jenny is in a bad temper. She snarls at the girl.

JENNY: Turn. I said *turn*. The other way.

Louise is getting very upset, but Jenny, who is indulging her own ill temper, does not notice: she has her head down, her mouth full of pins.

Louise changes posture, lifts one arm to touch the lampshade or fiddle with her hair.

JENNY: Don't do that! It alters the whole hang of the thing.

Louise bursts into tears.

LOUISE: Why are you being so horrible to me? *I* haven't done anything.

Jenny is horrified. She climbs onto the table and puts her arms round Louise. Their heads bump the lampshade.

FADE TO BLACK

PART FOUR

ONE MONTH EARLIER
DECEMBER 1984

It is a summer evening. In the entrance hall of City Girls' High, senior students in uniform are welcoming and directing next year's intake and their parents.

Jim is standing inside the door.

Louise sees him and comes bouncing up. Behind her are Kelly, Jenny, Chris and Malcolm.

We see from the nature of their greetings that the two families are no more than casually acquainted with each other.

Malcolm stands with folded arms and a carefully neutral expression.

In the entrance hall there is a mural, painted perhaps by an Old Girl of the school: mythical female figures, Pallas Athene in her helmet, nymphs, girls holding test tubes, girls hurling javelins, girls reading. All the characters in it are dressed in vague robes of indeterminate period.

Jim and Jenny, moving towards the assembly hall, mutter to each other.

JENNY: It's so old-fashioned it's almost feminist.

They all enter the hall. We see a proscenium arch stage with red curtains pulled back, a lectern, a microphone, several chairs in a row.

The hall is full of stackable seating, the kind whose seats flap into up-position with a very loud noise. The walls are covered in shields and honour boards. In strategic spots hang oil paintings of dignified old women, all of them in academic gowns, with severe expressions and folded hands.

Our characters sit in a row, Louise and Kelly side by side in the middle. Beside Jenny sits a stranger, a woman, who catches her eye and smiles. The woman keeps turning and looking over her shoulder.

WOMAN (*whispers to Jenny*): I think my ex-husband's going to turn up. With his new lady.

They grimace and laugh.

JENNY (*politely*): Do you live far?

WOMAN: Oh God, yes, miles away. Rebecca'll have to travel nearly three hours a day.

The Principal, wearing a suit, is clapping her hands for silence at the lectern.

She is a rather parodic figure: a bit of a Mrs Thatcher

in appearance and dress but *not posh*—her accent is like Edna Everage's, broad but with pretensions to gentility. Her manner is condescending to the point of rudeness: she addresses the adults as if they were students. Behind her, on the chairs, sit three other women, two oldish with short grey perms, one about thirty, rather chic, more modern-looking: the upper echelons of the staff hierarchy.

PRINCIPAL: Will those latecomers at the back please move quickly to their seats? We like to start our occasions on time at City Girls' High School.

A seat whacks sharply at the back.
 The woman next to Jenny, hearing the seat whack, cranes her neck towards back of hall.

WOMAN: Oh God, it's him.

She sinks down in her seat, almost giggling with nerves.

JENNY (*gazing at the Principal*): Isn't she *incredible*.

The woman turns around. Other parents are having trouble keeping a straight face.
 Kelly and Louise are staring intently at the Principal.

PRINCIPAL: Good evening ladies, gentlemen and students, and welcome. Congratulations to all those girls who've been successful in our entrance examinations. We know that the high standards we've set and maintained at City Girls' will be an inspiration to our incoming students. City Girls' has a long and very special tradition.

197

LOUISE (*out of the corner of her mouth*): There's a picture of the first woman surgeon in the state, up there.

KELLY: Are there any famous singers?

PRINCIPAL: Our students are privileged people, and, as we all know, privilege entails a corresponding responsibility. This is a demanding school. We ask a great deal of our girls and we expect the support of parents as well. Of course this may not suit everyone. If you don't like it here you don't have to stay.

An uncomfortable laugh.

———————

Eventually, the Principal sits down, and a small madrigal group files onto the stage to sing. It is old-fashioned; some of the girls are dags, but others have fashionable, extreme haircuts; all are taking the difficult music seriously, and singing it well.

　　Louise and Kelly are intent.

———————

That night, Malcolm drives home. He sits in silence, but Kelly and Chris are talking excitedly.

———————

KELLY: Two hours of homework a *night*! In year *nine*!

CHRIS (*with an excited laugh*): By year twelve you'll be
   working till two o'clock in the morning!

Chris gradually becomes aware that Malcolm is brooding,
not just thinking about something else.

CHRIS: What did you think of it, Malcolm?

MALCOLM: That woman was like a man in drag.

Kelly laughs, still unaware. But Chris has immediately
picked up his tone, and glances at him nervously.

MALCOLM: I'm not at all sure about this idea. If I'd known
   it was like that I wouldn't have let her sit for the exam.

KELLY: Like what?

MALCOLM: It's reactionary! It's elitist! That old battle-axe—
   the way she talked down to us. I take offence at being
   spoken to like that.

CHRIS (*daringly*): You won't have to. You're not the one
   going there.

He does not like *her* tone, either.
   A silence.

KELLY (*earnestly*): I liked the school, Malcolm. I did. I really liked it. And so did Louise.

CHRIS: And you must admit the music was marvellous.

MALCOLM: This is the end of the twentieth century! Why are they still singing that stuff? They should be letting them play rock 'n' roll. Anyway, a concert doesn't give you any idea of the kind of teaching they do. They should have an open day, so we can walk around and watch the kids learning to work computers.

KELLY: But that'd be really *boring*.

MALCOLM: What's so bloody special about City Girls', anyway?

KELLY: You heard what she said! They make you work! King Street's a bludge.

MALCOLM: Kids shouldn't have to be 'made to work'. They should be allowed to work at their own pace.

A silence.

KELLY: Malcolm. I really, really want to go. I want to be with Louise.

Pause.

MALCOLM: I'll think about it.

Silence. Chris and Kelly are looking at him.

MALCOLM (*under pressure; shouts*): I said I'll *think* about it!

A summer afternoon. In Jenny's backyard, the two girls are hanging out the clothes.

Louise works sloppily and lazily, bunging the pegs in anywhere on the garment, while Kelly does it properly with efficient movements and not pegging things by the collar; she is thinking of the ironing later.

KELLY: When are you going to ask her?

LOUISE: After tea.

That evening, Louise is playing the piano. Kelly is clearing the table. Jenny is watching the news on TV.

KELLY: Are you having a Christmas tree?

JENNY: No. ⎫
⎬ simultaneously
LOUISE: Yes. ⎭

JENNY: I'm not buying one. I hate them. It's just another rook. And they drop their needles everywhere.

LOUISE (*eagerly*): We could get one of those plastic ones from the service station. They're only $7.

KELLY: Malcolm says we're not going to give each other any presents this year.

LOUISE: But that's *disgusting*! How *mean*! Don't you think so, Mum?

JENNY (*shrugs, reluctant to undermine authority*): Everyone's got their own ideas.

KELLY: It's because of the Third World.

LOUISE (*picks up the ukelele and plays a little tune. Sings in grotesque parody of a C&W accent*):
    'Gonna have a party
    Dew you wanna come?
    If yew wanna come
    Yew better ask y' Mom'—
Hey Mum, can Kelly stay?

JENNY: All right, you be in bed by ten.

LOUISE: Ten-thirty.

JENNY: Ten-fifteen. No later.

The same evening. The girls are in the cupboard under the stairs of Jenny's house. Kelly holds a torch, Louise is burrowing in an open trunk, pulling out tinsel, baubles, stars, etc.

KELLY: Do you think she'll let us? She doesn't like parties much, does she.

LOUISE: She'll let us if we promise to clean up afterwards. Anyway when you change schools at our age you have to have some kind of celebration. How about this green stuff?

Pulls an old cotton curtain out of the trunk.

Several days later. It's the last day of third term. Outside the high school, a grand scene of farewell.

Louise and Kelly are saying goodbye. They and several girlfriends work themselves into a passion of tears, as if they will never see each other again.

Many kids pass. Some look at the melodramatic scene.

RENATO (*passing with another boy*): They're all lesos at City Girls' High.

KELLY: Charming.

Renato's friend, seeing the tragic farewells, remarks to Renato in genuine surprise:

FRIEND: They only live round the corner—they'll see each other every day.

———————

Days later. Early in the evening, Jenny enters her lounge room, and sees the Christmas tree the girls have made: an umbrella opened and wedged with bricks into a plastic bucket, with an old green curtain spread over it, its brass rings not quite concealed. A sparkly star on the umbrella's point. Paper chains, camels, moons, wise men and parcels are pinned to the curtain. They have even cleaned up: the bin is overflowing with paper scraps. On the table, two pairs of scissors, a roll of sticky tape, a bottle of Clag.

Jenny stands looking at this. Their eager, good-humoured ingenuity, after her mean-spiritedness: she is ashamed, and moved.

———————

Early evening, several days later, at Jenny's place.

Louise and Kelly are engaged in feverish preparation for the party. They have arranged the lounge room in a stiff way: dining chairs at regular intervals, along the wall, the table in the middle with food and glasses. The Christmas tree in evidence. Jenny enters.

The girls look at her, waiting for her approval: their anxiety is touching.

LOUISE: Is it all right?

KELLY: Does it look welcoming?

LOUISE: But what about the tree. It's pathetic.

JENNY: It's beautiful, girls.

We see her slight hesitation but they don't. Kelly stands up close to Jenny as if waiting for a hug. Jenny puts one arm round her shoulders.

The girls seem childish in their eagerness.

KELLY: Arkh! The sausage rolls.

Louise rushes off to the kitchen. Kelly moves away from Jenny and goes to the open window. She hangs out of it and looks up and down the street, then turns back to the room.

KELLY: What's the time?

JENNY: Half-past seven.

KELLY: That's the time we *said*. Nobody's here yet. What

if no one comes? Do you think we should start ringing them up?

JENNY: They'll come. Nobody ever arrives on time at a party—it's uncool.

A knock at the door.
    Louise and Kelly go stampeding past Jenny to answer.

———————————

Kelly and Louise rush to the front door and open it.
    On the doorstep stands Soula, a smiling Greek girl, all dressed up, carrying a plate covered in silver foil. Her brother Con is behind her on the footpath, delivering her. Shrieks of greeting.

LOUISE: Hi, Soula! Come in! You're the first one!

KELLY: Hi, Con.

CON (*completely uninterested*): I'll be back at eleven. I don't want to hang around, Soula. You be ready.

SOULA: Okay.

Soula comes in. The door is closed. Mass movement towards the lounge room. Jenny fights through in the opposite direction.

JENNY: I'm going for a little walk. I'll be back in an hour, all right?

No one is listening. She goes out the front door.

It's still very light—summer time, a pleasant evening. Jenny walks slowly along the street. She is relieved to be out of the tension of their expectation.

A quiet scene. Not much traffic. A few people sitting on doorsteps. Jenny turns a corner.

At Alison's front gate, Alison is leaning against the fence talking to Jenny, in the warm evening.

JENNY: They've got it set up like a dentist's waiting room. I felt like bursting into tears.

They laugh.

ALISON: Thank God we're old.

Wally flies past on a BMX without looking up.

JENNY: Isn't Wally speaking to you?

ALISON: I made him wear a helmet.

They lean there watching the kids on bikes, the odd skateboard.

ALISON: You long for them to have something as simple as a bad dream, so you can comfort them.

———————

Half an hour later, Jenny and Alison walk towards Jenny's front gate. The door is open and they go in.

———————

Inside the house, Alison goes straight up the stairs, to the lavatory.

From the lounge room, sounds of a dispute.

Jenny enters the lounge room. A scene of minor bedlam, which freezes as she appears.

Kelly is on the sofa with Renato. They are pashing-on in a flamboyant exhibitionist style.

Soula and four other girls are clustered in a corner, embarrassed, giggling.

Louise, looking anxious, runs in from the kitchen and stops dead at the sight of her mother.

JENNY: What's going on?

Renato hears her, and flees out the front way. Kelly sits up, stunned with kissing.

Louise begins to give a flustered report: she's afraid Jenny will be angry.

LOUISE: We invited some boys from school—but they sort of broke in, and they pinched the champagne out of the fridge when I wasn't looking. I couldn't stop them.

Louise is almost in tears. The other girls, relieved to see an authority figure, move closer.

Jenny goes into the kitchen and sees the fridge door open, plundered. She closes it as she passes.

Jenny continues out the back door and sees three boys, much less brazen than Renato, loitering outside the back gate. Two empty (cheap) champagne bottles are lying in the gutter. The boys take off when they see her, but stop again twenty yards away and watch to see what Jenny will do. They are muttering to each other and laughing.

BOY (*daringly*): Youse are slack.

Jenny ignores him. She picks up the empty bottles and stands them next to the gate. She goes into the kitchen and shuts the back door.

———————

Upstairs, a toilet flushes and Alison walks out of the bathroom. She goes to the stairs and hangs over the bannister, wondering what's keeping Jenny.

———————

Meanwhile, in the lounge room, though it's a warm night, the girls are closing the window and pulling the blinds and curtains across.

Kelly is still sitting quietly on the couch.

Jenny enters from the kitchen. She and Kelly look at each other without speaking; Kelly's expression is inscrutable, but Jenny's is curious, almost respectful. Kelly gives a very small smile.

LOUISE: I'm going to lock the front door.

She runs off down the hallway. Jenny turns and follows behind. Louise closes the door to a crack. She speaks to someone outside. Jenny is listening.

LOUISE (*through the crack*): At the very least I think you owe me an apology, Renato.

She slams the door and turns round. She sees Jenny watching her.

LOUISE: It's *hopeless* with boys. It's a waste of time to invite them. They're just *hopeless*.

She walks briskly past Jenny towards the lounge room.

———————————

An hour later, Alison lounges on Jenny's bed, cutting her toenails. Jenny is standing at the open window looking out.

The dull, endless thumping of the bass from the girls' party below: sometimes it stops, then immediately begins again.

The women are drinking vodka. Jenny is eating peanuts out of a packet while she is watching an argument in the street and reporting its progress to Alison, who does not look up but makes murmured comments.

JENNY: Oh no. He's crying. He's got a big white hanky in his hand.

Pause.

Sound of a car door being slammed.

JENNY: She's going back to her own car.

Another car door bangs.

JENNY: She's locking herself in. Oh my God. He's trying to open the door. Ah—she's letting him in the passenger side.

ALISON (*not looking up*): Is there going to be violence?

JENNY: She's trying to leave him. He loves her. She's breaking his heart. Oh my God. She's banging her head against the steering wheel. He's getting out. She's driving away. They're *waving* to each other.

Pause.

JENNY: Now he's getting back into *his* car. He's lighting a cigarette. He's not starting the motor. He's just sitting there.

ALISON: Just as well. The state he's in. There'd be carnage on the roads.

Jenny leans out the window and shouts.

JENNY: Time heals, mate! I'm forty, and I know!

ALISON (*laughing*): Shutup! He'll hear you!

JENNY: He's got the windows rolled up.

Alison gets off the bed and goes to the window. Jenny makes room for her and they lean side by side on the sill, looking out into the summer night. The street is full of parked cars. They drink.

A burst of laughter and rhythmical stamping from downstairs.

———————————

Down in the lounge room, the windows and blinds are shut tight. The girls' faces are shiny with sweat and make-up. They have dragged out the dress-up trunk and are all attired in exaggerated outfits, clunky cork-soled wedgies, sequined tops; some are dressed as men. Loud music.

They are barricaded in and are having a wonderful time: a last glorious burst of *childhood*.

Kelly is joining in with gusto. She leaps up on the table and dances. A tremendous noise.

After midnight in Jenny's lounge room. The lights are on. Nobody is there. The wreckage of the party.

The window is open.

A paper cup rolls across the table, pushed by the wind.

Two days later, in the afternoon, Jenny is down on her knees in the bathroom, scrubbing out the shower with Ajax. She is whistling and singing.

Sound of running feet in the street outside. The back gate bangs, the door slams. Feet running up the stairs.

LOUISE (*voice-over*): Mum? Mum!

JENNY (*stands up*): I'm in here.

Kelly and Louise burst in. They are both out of breath. Kelly's face is puffed up from crying. Louise is panting with importance and outrage.

LOUISE: Mum! Malcolm's changed his mind.

JENNY: About what?

LOUISE: He won't let Kelly go.

Jenny still holding the sponge, stares at them, not understanding.

KELLY: He won't let me go to City Girls'.

She begins to cry again.

JENNY: But you passed the exam. You got in.

LOUISE: He doesn't care about that. He's changed his mind. He hated the Orientation Night and now he won't let her go. Mum, can't you do something?

JENNY (*still stunned*): What can *I* do?

LOUISE: Talk to him! Go and see him! He'll listen to you.

JENNY: No he won't. He doesn't even know me.

LOUISE: That doesn't matter.

Louise bursts into tears. They are terribly worked up.

JENNY: But Kelly—surely your mother—

Kelly just shakes her head.

LOUISE: Oh *please*, Mum—can't you help us?

JENNY: Look, sweetheart, I don't see how I can. It'd only make things worse if *I* stuck my nose in. He'd say it was none of my business.

LOUISE (*in a passion*): Oh, it's so *unfair*. And they rejoiced with us when we passed the exam! They drank the champagne and everything! I *hate* him!

Kelly has stepped back, as if she holds out no hope from anybody.

Louise puts her arm around Kelly's waist (she can't reach her shoulder) and they walk away together, crying, with their heads down.

Jenny is left holding the Ajax and the Wettex.

Ten o'clock on Christmas morning.

A car pulls up at Jenny's front door.

Kelly gets out with a string bag and runs to the door. The engine keeps running. She knocks. Jim opens.

JIM (*surprised*): Why didn't you come round the back?

KELLY: Merry Christmas, Jim.

She rummages in her string bag and produces a small parcel—it looks as if it contains a pencil. Jim is very surprised and stands looking at it.

Kelly passes him and goes into the house.

The same morning. Under the home-made tree, Louise is opening parcels, with Jenny.

Kelly enters, with Jim behind her.

KELLY: Hullo.

They greet her. Everyone is quiet.

LOUISE: There's some presents for you here! Did you get any at home?

KELLY: Mum gave me a beach towel. I can't stay. They're waiting in the car. We're going to Nanna's.

Kelly looks subdued. Louise rounds up the parcels for her. Kelly unloads her two parcels, one for Jenny, and one for Louise. They contain small cheap objects but have been carefully wrapped.

Jenny leaves the room.

LOUISE: Did you talk to him?

216

KELLY (*shrugs*): It's no good. He only yells at me, and then he starts fighting with Mum.

Louise is helpless. She'd like to comfort but doesn't know how.

Jenny returns while they are speaking. She leans towards Louise's pile of presents and discreetly removes the tag from a little wrapped box, then turns to Kelly and hands it to her.

JENNY: Here, Kelly. This is for you.

Kelly takes the box, surprised, and opens it. Inside are some blue dangly earrings that Louise had wanted. Kelly kisses Jenny: she looks a bit stunned.

KELLY: I *love* them.

We see Louise's face: she is devastated. It is a pointless gesture on Jenny's part.

FADE TO BLACK

PART FIVE

TWO MONTHS EARLIER
OCTOBER 1984

It is almost midday: a spring morning.

In a classroom at City Girls' High School, an exam is in progress. Rows of thirteen- and fourteen-year-old girls (some in street clothes, some in uniforms of different schools—not a homogeneous group—among them quite a few Chinese, Greeks and Italians) are all slaving away. A tense silence. The teacher (a woman in her fifties) walks up and down. The blackboard has times crossed off, up to 11.55.

Some keep scribbling. Others are checking their work. One or two are already sitting back with folded hands.

We see Kelly and Louise. Kelly is surrounded by screwed-up bits of paper and is still madly scribbling. Louise is reading through her answers: her desk is orderly but she is very tense, twiddling a lock of hair in one hand and chewing her pen.

TEACHER: Right, girls. Pens down.

A clatter, a sigh, a rustle.

One girl keeps scribbling. It is Soula.

TEACHER: Leave your papers folded with your names and schools clearly marked on the outside. You may go.

They stand up (still overawed by the unfamiliar surroundings) and file out. Kelly and Louise are among them, casting anxious looks back at Soula.

The teacher stands by the door as they pass.

Camera stays in the classroom.

Outside a swell of girls' voices, some shrieking, others going 'Shoosh'!

Soula is the last to get up, long after the others. Her tension and distress are terrible to see: not tears, but a frightful tightness which is worse.

———————

Out in the schoolyard, Soula runs through the crowd of girls toward a hot Commodore which is parked half up on the footpath. Con is leaning against it with his arms folded. He sees Soula coming and steps forward, dismayed at the state she is in.

Kelly and Louise watch her get into the car.

KELLY (*with real feeling*): Poor thing.

They watch the Commodore roar away, then turn to each other. The babble is going on behind them.

LOUISE: Did you finish?

KELLY: Yep. Did you?

LOUISE (*beginning to smile*): Yep.

KELLY: What essay topic did you do?

LOUISE: I did 'The Most Unusual Person I Have Ever Met'.

KELLY: Who'd you write about?

LOUISE: You, actually.

KELLY: Argh! You did not! You dag!

She grabs Louise's cheeks, pinches her and shakes her head like a grandmother with a baby that she is loving half to death.

They are both laughing with the release of tension.

Some nights later Kelly and Louise are ensconced on the couch in Jenny's lounge room, their legs wrapped in a rug. Both are weeping luxuriously, chewing chocolate. A box of Kleenex stands between them, on the low table, beside a plate of snacks.

Swelling music from the TV indicates the end of *Gone with the Wind*.

Louise presses the remote button and there is silence. Kelly blows her nose and heaves a quivering sigh. They are both fat-eyed and red-nosed.

KELLY: Wasn't it *gorgeous*.

LOUISE: That's the fifth time I've seen it.

More quivering breaths and blowing of noses.

LOUISE: I love the book. When I read it at Grandma's, I cried so much my pillow was all wet. I cried really loudly. I went 'er her her!'

They both start again—'Er her her'—half mocking themselves, half really bawling.

KELLY: How did they stand those *corsets*.

LOUISE: 'Whah Scow-leyett! Ever'body knows yew got the littlest waist in th' en-tah county!'

Kelly is reading the TV guide. She reaches for the plate of food.

KELLY: 12.45—*Rear Window*. That's got Grace Kelly in it. Would you contemplate a smoked oyster on a biscuit?

She hands Louise a biscuit with several smoked oysters stacked on it.

Upstairs in her bedroom, Jenny has fallen asleep with the light on, the book on her chest.

Saturday afternoon at North Head. Jenny is standing by a clump of bushes. No one else is in sight. She is looking to left and right as if keeping watch.

JENNY: There's no one coming! Just *do* it!

LOUISE (*from behind the bushes*): Well turn around, can't you?

Jenny does so. At the top of the path a man appears and shouts to a sullen teenage boy who slouches into view lower down the path. Jenny is between them.

JASON'S DAD: Jason! Will you please *keep up*?

Jason slummocks past at a dogtrot, hands in pockets. Does not look at Jenny as he passes.

Louise scrambles up out of the bushes.

LOUISE: That was close! He nearly saw me.

They walk along the path to the edge of the cliff.

JENNY: When are *you* going to rebel?

LOUISE (*surprised*): Don't you think I rebel enough?

JENNY: Aren't teenagers supposed to?

LOUISE (*clicks her tongue*): 'Teenagers'. Don't embarrass me. You talk like a magazine.

Pause.
　　They look at the sea.

JENNY: Would you say Kelly was rebelling?

Louise shrugs as if reluctant to answer.

JENNY: Kelly's more interested in boys and sex than you are, isn't she.

LOUISE: Oh shutup! Do we have to talk about this?

JENNY (*persisting*): But you will *tell* me when you start getting your period, won't you?

LOUISE: Shutup, Mum! You're *revolting*.

Jenny, embarrassed and laughing, tries to put her arm round Louise, who darts away.

LOUISE (*calls back to her*): If you really want to know something, Kelly's on the pill.

Louise waits a few yards away for Jenny to catch up. They walk. Jenny picks up a twig and strips it.

JENNY: Does Kelly actually *do* it?

LOUISE (*mortified with embarrassment*): How would *I* know? You're so awful! You stick your nose into everybody's business.

JENNY: But that's what the pill's *for*, isn't it?

LOUISE: I wish I hadn't told you. I wish I never told you *any*thing. Don't you dare tell.

They stump along. It is a beautiful spring day.

———————

Afternoon.

A hand with a biro is writing on a lined pad in big sprawling letters: 'Dear Sir'. It is Kelly's hand.

Kelly and Louise are sitting at a desk in an empty classroom of their old high school. Kelly scribbles out the last few lines. They think. Louise eats some CC's out of an open packet on the desk.

A cleaner comes in and starts to rub off the blackboard: he's a Greek in a boilersuit.

KELLY: We'll have to do it again, in best writing.

LOUISE: Read out what we've got so far.

KELLY (*reads*): 'To the editor. We are two young girls, who do not wish to die. Our lives are before us. We want to study, to learn about the world. But every time we open the newspaper . . .'

LOUISE: 'We read about the arms race.'

Kelly writes.

KELLY: 'Mr Reagan and Mr—' What's the Russian president called?

LOUISE: Haven't they got a new one?

KELLY: We should know that.

LOUISE: Do you think we should say about nuclear stuff right at the beginning?

KELLY (*reads*): 'We are two young girls. Who do not wish to die.'

225

The cleaner begins to mop the floor. As he works he sings, very softly, one of those Greek songs with many flourishes that sound strange and difficult to us.

———————

It is later the same afternoon, in a corridor of the school building, empty except for Kelly and Louise who are heading along it, going home.

LOUISE: Wait for me.

Dumps bag and darts into dunny.
    Kelly waits.
    Pause.
    Louise shouts from inside.

LOUISE (*voice-over*): Kelly! Come here! Quick!

Kelly runs into the toilets.
    A girl's legs are sticking out under the half-open door of one cubicle. She is face down. Louise is bending over her, trying to drag her out and roll her over.
    The girl is tall, much bigger than either of the girls: at least sixteen, seventeen years.
    She has vomited.
    Louise tugs at her, not knowing what to do.

KELLY: Do you know how to do mouth-to-mouth?

226

LOUISE (*disgusted*): But she's spewed!

The girl starts to come to. She drags herself to her feet, and staggers to the dunny to press the flush button.

Kelly and Louise stand back, alarmed and impressed.

KELLY: Are you all right?

The girl gives them a contemptuous look. She goes to the basin, tears off a length of paper towel and begins to sponge the vomit off her white trousers.

GIRL: Piss off.

At the door, Kelly turns to the girl.

KELLY (*with heavy sarcasm*): Excuse *me*.

They bolt; their bags thump.

———————————

Outside, Louise and Kelly walk away across the empty yard.

LOUISE: She must be drunk.

KELLY: Maybe she's a drug addict.

LOUISE (*shocked*): Do they spew?

KELLY: She didn't smell like a drunk.

They walk in silence.

LOUISE: I'm *never* going to use drugs. I'm never even going to smoke.

Looking at this prim little figure, we can believe it.

LOUISE: It's *disgusting*.

Kelly walks along without answering. She is pondering what she has seen. While Louise simply and ignorantly rejects it, Kelly is more curious, and thinks about it. Louise glances at Kelly who does not notice.

Morning, several days later.

Jenny is in her car, driving towards Louise's school.

She turns the corner, and the school comes into view. The street is empty, except for Louise standing in front of a milkbar opposite the school, and on a bench twenty feet away from her, a couple pashing on shamelessly, hard at it. Louise is studiously ignoring them.

Jenny pulls up. Louise runs across the road to the car. Jenny winds the window down and hands Louise a locker key and a paper bag of lunch.

LOUISE: Thanks, Mum. Sorry.

228

JENNY: Isn't that Kelly?

Louise barely glances at the kissing couple.

LOUISE: Course it's not! She must be in Maths by now.
She'll be waiting for me. Bye.

Louise runs off.
Jenny does a U-turn. The couple unclasps. The girl is
not Kelly.

The same morning, in a classroom full of girls and boys.
A low hum of activity.
The teacher at the board is explaining a maths
problem. The room is modern, unlike the one where the
exam took place at City Girls': grey exposed bricks, and
the tables have blue laminex tops: the kind of high school
that's had money spent on its buildings.
Kelly with an empty seat beside her (Louise's) is writing
very fast. She has an open maths book on the desk as well—
an unfinished calculation. She is pouring out a great note
to Louise, writing carelessly in a sprawling hand. The top
sheet says: 'To my dearest friend Louise.' We see she has
already covered several foolscap sides: the text is sprinkled
with printed words, fast rough drawings, clumps of excla-
mation marks, etc.

KELLY (*voice-over*): 'To my dearest friend Louise,

Well to tell you the truth NO I have never received a letter that long—My God! All those pages how did you manage it? I'll try to make this long but I don't know exactly how long well your about to find out. I started this in art. I was so bored without you and now it's maths and even worse; where are you? I hope you aren't sick or been rushed to hospital in the middle of the night and no one told me. I would buy the sweetest flowers and put them by your bedside, lillies, roses, whatever thy heart couldest desire. Here is a picture of my nose that pimple is really saw. It is beginning to annoy me, quite a lot. Today is the day we will be told wether or not we got into City Girls'. I can't wait. If I don't get in I will kill myself I swear. I think we should each make a promise that if the other does not get in we will not go either. That's not very clear expression but you know what I mean. I just could not *bear* another four years in this hell-hole without you. My spelling is so bad. Do you think they take off marks for that? What if we got in but they didn't put us in the same class? Endless things to worry about so I am keeping my fingers crossed and holding my breath. This pen keeps konking out I've now tried about six or seven pens to find one that works. This pen is from the pizza shop in Canley, we all got one last year when Mr Papalco took us on the Italian excursion, remember? I realy have to buy some material today for my sewing class as I have only cut out the pattern and we are already into the second half of the term. A lady has just walked by with

230

a brolly, IT IS MEANT TO BE SPRING! Hurry up Louise, life has no meaning without you. Renato is bending over. He looks so cute in his little shorts—quite charming. I've come to the conclusion that he would make a very good *gay*! but for some reason Soula and I don't think he would let himself have anything to do with "men" but only time will tell. We watched a video last night called TESS. I have just finished reading the book so I was realy quite pleased to see it. Do you remember that kid called Tony, he used to hang out with Renato and them? He's really small and I can't say I'm all that fond of him well I'm invited to his party in a few weeks and I have doubts as to whether or not I will be going—If I don't I won't have missed out on much if you get my drift. I expect that rat Guy will be going which casts another dark shadow over it. Oh well. This is page number three, nothing compared to what you wrote. When are you going to be up at Pelican Beach? We should get it organised so that I can be up there when you are. I hope it's after Christmas what do you reckon? I can just tell that I'm going to get very very very burned e.g. as bright as a beetroot while as usual you will go brown in one day. You must be a wog, sorry, only joking. God I was scared before I went to the Family Planning Clinic. But it was okay after all. It was fairly impersonal. I'm a fairly routine case—nothing special so they had no reason for being astounded. Life rolls on. I realy want a job this summer Louise but I don't know if there is much chance of one. Never mind. Notice I am making my writing smaller so you get *more value*. Oh gosh Louise I realy

realy really realy want to live with my daddy. It must sound funny, me saying "Daddy" and not "Dad", but I just don't like "Dad". What's more it is *too common*. I just don't know if he will want me and if I will be allowed to. I realy need a change of environment. God you wouldn't believe how much I want to even though at times I have had him up the eyeballs but I really realy realy want to live with him. If he says yes the only barrier is Malcolm. He doesn't like Daddy so I think he will probably give me the third degree but I'm still hoping. It is just not fair. It would be so good to have my own room, my own space, something I have never had. I've been trying to work out the colour scheme but I just can't decide on a colour to paint the cupboard and to have for curtains. I hate to think about it in case it doesn't happen and yet I can't stop. Yipee! Yipee! Yipee! Hey man did you know that doodle blunk grandshun splonkle wunk blert danbrokmellop yefturd travoon goflarat? Lots of love from your best and most faithful friend Kelly.

PS now you're not the only one to have written a six-page letter so ner ner ner.'

She folds the letter rapidly, wraps it in another sheet of paper, scribbles *Louise* on the outside and slides it on to Louise's folder exactly as Louise gets back to her seat after getting the lunch and locker key from Jenny.

They look at each other. They are dying to laugh. They look at each other with *tenderness*.

Later the same afternoon.

Kelly and Louise are running down the street. They are leaping and screaming.

Behind them walks Jenny, smiling, carrying a paper bag with a bottle of champagne poking out the top.

They approach Kelly's house.

The front hall at Kelly's house: the door bursts open, and in barge the two girls and Jenny, all jubilant.

KELLY: We passed! We passed! We passed!

Chris runs out.

CHRIS: Shh! Shh! Malcolm's asleep!

They all mime dismay, and tiptoe down the hallway. A fluster of suppressed excitement. Before they can get to the kitchen Malcolm emerges like a bear with a sore head.

MALCOLM: What the bloody hell's all the fuss about?

CHRIS: The girls passed the exam, Mal. They got into City Girls' High School.

Malcolm makes a big effort.

MALCOLM: Good on you. Congratulations. I'll get my shoes on.

He goes out.

KELLY: Only us two! None of the others passed. Not even Soula.

LOUISE: Not even Julie—and not even *Justine*!

KELLY: Louise and me are the *only ones*!

The girls' excitement has got Chris and Jenny through the awkward social moment.

    Chris gets glasses, Jenny opens the bottle. Shrieks all round as it pops.

    Jenny fills the glasses.

    Malcolm comes back but stays leaning in the doorway, smiling, with his hands in his pockets.

LOUISE: What'll we drink to?

CHRIS: To the girls. To our clever girls.

The girls raise their glasses—but Kelly can't contain herself and drops back her head with a shriek of excitement and joy.

FREEZE ON THIS

THE END

All Those Tears
by Laura Jones

MOST OF US watch films but don't read screenplays. They are odd pieces of writing because they only exist in order to become something else. They necessarily 'vanish', as the screenwriter Jean-Claude Carrière has written. The process of production takes over, and the screenplay disappears, no longer needed, into the film.

I haven't seen these two films since they were released: *Two Friends* on my television screen in 1986, and *The Last Days of Chez Nous* in the cinema in 1992. Helen Garner was sitting behind me at a screening of *Chez Nous* for cast, crew and friends, and my consciousness of her was high—my sympathy for what it is like for a screenwriter to see the film made from their screenplay for the first time, with an audience. You are watching the radical transformation of your work.

After seeing the first film I wrote as part of an audience, I felt as if I had done a hard workout; my muscles ached.

After some shilly-shallying I decided not to re-watch *Two Friends* or *Chez Nous* but only to read the screenplays, as the first pieces of work in the film-making process yet to come. To imagine these films haven't been made is an almost impossible sleight of mind, but here they are, in front of me: the screenplays, on the page, Helen Garner's imagined films.

The story of *Two Friends* is daringly told in reverse chronology, backwards, although each of the five parts is told in the present tense, forwards. We hold these two storytelling modes in our minds at once, the forward momentum and the backwards knowledge. In a linear narrative, we expect to discover what happens next. Here, we discover what has just happened. This asks a lot of the viewer, and maybe even more of the reader, who has to become a detective within the screenplay. Such deft playing with time—elegant, formal and musical—offers great storytelling pleasure, as we move from dark to light, from the painful separation of two adolescent girls to the rapturous closeness of ten months earlier.

Although more screen time is given to the two fourteen-year-olds, Louise and Kelly, it's Louise's mother, Jenny, who is our guide—our compass—in their friendship. This mother–daughter relationship stays steady at the centre, and helps us chart the break-up of the friendship. It's they—the twosome of mother and daughter—who are left in the wake of the whirlwind that Kelly creates as she is forced to take off from home, from school, from Louise. It's a complex portrait of a mother and daughter: funny, painful, intimate, anxious, fearful, hopeful, with complicity and small betrayals, power shifts and passionate attachment. It reflects, although it is very different in nature, the passionate attachment between the girls.

Two Friends—unlike *The Last Days of Chez Nous*, where all the trouble is cooked up from within—has a villain. Malcolm, Kelly's stepfather, is a classic bully. The threat of violence hangs around him; he generates fear, obedience and appeasement in the women who live with him. Kelly's mother is 'like a prisoner'. Although Malcolm is a secondary character, it's his decision that turns the key of the drama. His lordly ruling creates the definitive split between the two girls: they now have two distinct paths. The injustice is like a cleaver within the narrative.

Malcolm is in the dark circle of other bullies in Australian fiction, along with Felix Shaw from Elizabeth Harrower's *The Watch Tower* and Sam Pollit from Christina Stead's *The Man Who Loved Children*. He enjoys his power, enjoys the pleading of Kelly and her mother, bides his time in doling out punishments. The incremental exertion of his powers makes us shudder.

As *Two Friends* ends on its vivid note of 'excitement and joy'—Helen Garner asks us to imagine a freeze frame on this image—we know instantly that the joy will be (has been!) destroyed. In that second we know it doesn't last; it has unspooled. Were the screenplay to hit a wrong note in its reverse chronology, the whole thing would fall apart. But these delicate notes, these scenes and larger movements, play out within a robust, sure-footed structure.

An unanswered question hangs in the narrative of *Two Friends*: would Louise and Kelly, in the course of time and without Malcolm's intrusion, break up? Kelly is already on the path to sexual adventures, while for Louise sex is still a mystery. We see Kelly out of her depth when she visits her father for the night and encounters his friend Kevin. When things go too far, too fast, she flees and takes refuge with Jenny and Louise. Kelly has entered into knowledge that Louise can't share, and it's Kelly and Jenny who—with their 'perfect, wordless understanding'—are complicit in keeping it from Louise, who is more 'innocent than either of them'.

The next scene moves swiftly to the two girls in bed, and ends on Kelly's touching 'Shh. Go to sleep.' The juxtaposing of the two beds—Kelly in bed with Kevin at her father's flat, and Kelly in bed with Louise, snuggling up for sleep—gives us the affecting, subtle balancing of scenes that creates a double portrait of one girl stepping out into the world of experience and the other remaining, just, in childhood.

The friendship between Louise and Kelly has some of the intensity, the constantly shifting laws of strength and weakness, of the friendship between Lila and Elena in Elena Ferrante's novel *My Brilliant Friend*. A passionate friendship is the same in Naples in the 1950s as it is in Sydney in the 1980s, although in vastly different social worlds. I had a friendship like this; my daughter also had one. Perhaps the nature of these friendships never changes, and that is one of the reasons *Two Friends* seems so real and alive to a reader in 2016.

*

All the weeping, all the tears, all the crying, in both screenplays: I've never read so many tears. Hot tears of adolescence; tears of betrayal; tears of humiliation; tears of anger; tears of fear;

tears of loss; tears of grief; tears of lost friendship—a lost sister, husband, best friend. But these screenplays are also very funny. There are few screenwriters who can so easily—so artfully—imbue ambiguous, painful moments with humour. These scenes never falter in their twin purpose.

Both *The Last Days of Chez Nous* and *Two Friends* are about last days. *Chez Nous* opens with the return of Vicki, the prodigal sister. Vicki, the beloved, is the catalyst for the household breaking up. As Malcolm does in *Two Friends*, Vicki turns the key of the drama; but the fault lines are already laid in the marriage between Vicki's older sister, Beth, and her French husband, JP. Unlike Malcolm, Vicki is not a villain: there are no villains, no heroes, in this world. Beth's sixteen-year-old daughter, Annie, and Tim, a student who comes to rent a room in the house, are the innocents—a little steady flame in the dramas of the adults.

Beth—or Bef, as JP's accent makes her—is a gift of a character for an actor: she lurches, she runs, she hurries, she darts; she is brisk, bossy, vigorous. Every time she is described, her activity is full-on. Beth lists her failings to JP: 'Do you think I need to be *told* I'm not lovable? I *know* that! I know what I'm like! I'm bossy, impatient, too motherly, ill-mannered, unfaithful, greedy, a spend-thrift.' She is one of the most subtle and devastating woman characters written for Australian film.

Beth rules the roost because she's the bossy, capable one. The others cede this territory to her; that's her way, and they accept it. Small rebellions. Bigger stoushes. Until they come into their own while Beth is away with her father on a road trip into the desert. When Beth returns she understands she has lost control of the house; a power shift has taken place; things are now up for grabs. We have read the scenes in the house intercut with the scenes in the desert, so we know her sister and her husband have become lovers—but Beth doesn't, and we watch her intuition get to work when she returns.

Chez Nous has its own laws of strength and weakness; it is in a distinctly different key from *Two Friends*. Close to the end of *Chez Nous*, Beth says of Vicki, 'I used to love her so much it hurt me to look at her.' Beth's closeness to her sister mirrors the closeness of Louise and Kelly in *Two Friends*. With both, there is a crucial third figure: JP in *Chez Nous*, and Jenny in *Two Friends*. It's these constantly shifting power dynamics—there's often someone on the outer in a threesome—that the screenplays take the measure of.

There are hijinks and games all the way through *Chez Nous*, at least until the break-up of the house is underway and the tone shifts to a more discordant key—of recognition, grief, loss, pain, anger and separation. There is no melodrama; all these emotions are tempered with a sharp lack of sentimentality in the writing. But the games! Cards; colouring-in; a joke with plastic dog shit; JP's beret, thrown like a frisbee: these show us the daily domestic pleasures of the household. They are a light refrain to its deeper rumblings and fissures.

There is a game that Beth, Vicki and Annie play: the Butterworths. It is a different order of game to the jokes and hijinks. The last time we see the Butterworths is in a crucial scene—a lunch intended to celebrate JP's Australian citizenship—where the three women are judged by their friend Angelo: 'You lot are sick.' It is a game others can't join in, or get the hang of. JP calls it 'anti working-class', without understanding the exhilarating, compulsive way the three women fall into the Butterworth characters. It is during this last playing of the Butterworths that Beth 'drops her bundle', and says to the table: 'It's not anti-anything. I wish I was like Cheryl [Butterworth]. Cheryl's better than me. She's rough as bags, but she's got more heart.'

Chez Nous takes place in one main location: the house. Although we leave it for some scenes—JP's citizenship ceremony; a local café, a couple of times; an abortion clinic—the house, and the life of the street immediately outside, forms the world of the narrative. This creates a narrow storytelling focus, so when we go with Beth and her father on their unprecedented road trip it is a marked shift in tone: there is a big breathing space. The desert and its mysteries—the outback, where Beth hopes to 'find something', and to see if she and her father can talk without squabbling—is profoundly different: 'They walk, arm in arm. The sky is absolutely swimming with stars. The silence is tremendous.'

This moment in the desert, with Beth and her father's talk about God, is twinned in the screenplay with the cypress trees seen in the distance from the house. Both hold a mystery, a meaning beyond the quotidian. The cypress trees are the other, Proust's lost paradise in inner-city Melbourne, the apprehended but not yet found. Beth tells her friend Sally: 'I've been up and down those lanes, and I can never find them.' The screenplay ends with Vicki and JP having left to live together; Annie and Tim at the piano, practising 'Donna Lee'; and Beth walking away from the house, towards the cypress trees. She can see the dark shapes of their tops, 'like a hand held up', in the distance.

It's an open ending: we don't know if Beth finds the trees, or if she is again diverted. As I read the ending, I feel—just outside the circle of the story—that Beth finds the trees; she arrives there. But another ending outside the circle seems entirely possible: she is diverted, or can't quite find the spot, and the cypress trees continue to be the other for which she searches.

*

Helen Garner's novels and short stories hovered in the back of my mind as I re-read these screenplays. The angel in *Cosmo Cosmolino* (1992) is a boldly direct take on the other, the cypress trees, in *Chez Nous*—and I remember the novel was published at around the same time that the film was released. Once I started to think of the screenplays as part of the larger landscape of Garner's writing, I was dazzled: I saw a world where every piece is satisfyingly complete and distinctive, but all hang together as a whole.

Across the novels, stories and screenplays the characters age; their concerns change. The children grow up, leave home; there are deaths; the big shared households shrink; and in Garner's most recent novel, *The Spare Room* (2008), a woman in her sixties, living alone, looks after a dying friend. There is—very affectingly, for me—the sense of living with these characters over time. Not in the intricately patterned manner of long novel cycles such as Anthony Powell's *A Dance to the Music of Time*; it's not the purpose, I imagine, of any one of Garner's fictions to be part of a sequence, but they do have this deeply pleasing cumulative effect.

The screenplays inhabit the same fictional world as the novels: the cobbled-together, shifting households; music running through everything, so natural as to be like breathing; children, always so astonishingly written. The houses, all the houses: order made out of chaos, or a few orderly rooms holding chaos at bay. Keynotes of resilience, hope, humour, countering broken spirits, resignation, grief. Betrayals bringing grief, and also relief; the splitting-up of twosomes, the combustible spikiness of threesomes. The effect on characters of light, air, storms, clouds; vivid tableaux; barely there thresholds between house and street.

With some exceptions, such as *Monkey Grip* (1977), Part 1 of *Cosmo Cosmolino* and some of the stories in *Postcards from Surfers* (1985), Garner's fiction allows us access to each character in intimate third person: points of view bounce with ease, sometimes with audacious speed, as in *The Children's Bach* (1984)—just as the screenplays do. The screenplays have a tighter focus than Garner's other fictions. They have a different purpose: they are written for performance and visual storytelling. They are to be seen differently, absorbed differently. But, like the novels, they are a joy to read.

Text Classics

Dancing on Coral
Glenda Adams
Introduced by Susan Wyndham

The True Story of Spit MacPhee
James Aldridge
Introduced by Phillip Gwynne

The Commandant
Jessica Anderson
Introduced by Carmen Callil

Homesickness
Murray Bail
Introduced by Peter Conrad

Sydney Bridge Upside Down
David Ballantyne
Introduced by Kate De Goldi

Bush Studies
Barbara Baynton
Introduced by Helen Garner

Between Sky & Sea
Herz Bergner
Introduced by Arnold Zable

The Cardboard Crown
Martin Boyd
Introduced by Brenda Niall

A Difficult Young Man
Martin Boyd
Introduced by Sonya Hartnett

Outbreak of Love
Martin Boyd
Introduced by Chris Womersley

When Blackbirds Sing
Martin Boyd
Introduced by Chris Wallace-Crabbe

The Australian Ugliness
Robin Boyd
Introduced by Christos Tsiolkas

All the Green Year
Don Charlwood
Introduced by Michael McGirr

They Found a Cave
Nan Chauncy
Introduced by John Marsden

textclassics.com.au